CU00676565

The Adventures of Gurudeva

SEEPERSAD NAIPAUL

The Adventures
of Gurudeva

With a Foreword by V. S. Naipaul

HEINEMANN : LONDON

First published in Great Britain 1976 by
André Deutsch Limited
This edition published 1995
by William Heinemann Ltd
an imprint of Reed Consumer Books Ltd
Michelin House, 81 Fulham Road, London SW3 6RB
and Auckland, Melbourne, Singapore and Toronto

A CIP catalogue record for this title
is available from the British Library
ISBN 0 434 00284 4

Typeset by CentraCet Limited, Cambridge
Printed and bound in Great Britain
by Clays Ltd., St Ives plc

Foreword

The shorter stories or pieces that were published earlier with The Adventures of Gurudeva *have been left out of this edition, and a few small adjustments have had to be made to the foreword.*

I

My father, Seepersad Naipaul, who was a journalist on the *Trinidad Guardian* for most of his working life, published a small collection of his short stories in Trinidad in 1943. He was thirty-seven; he had been a journalist off and on for fourteen years and had been writing stories for five. The booklet he put together, some seventy pages long, was called *Gurudeva and other Indian Tales*; and it was my introduction to book-making. The printing was done, slowly, by the Guardian Commercial Printery; my father brought the proofs home bit by bit in his jacket pocket; and I shared his hysteria when the linotypists, falling into everyday ways, set – permanently, as it turned out – two of the stories in narrow newspaper-style columns.

The book, when it was published, drew one or two letters

of abuse from people who thought that my father had written damagingly of our Indian community. There also came a letter many pages long, closely written in inks of different colours, the handwriting sloping this way and that, from a religion-crazed Muslim. This man later bought space in the *Trinidad Guardian* to print his photograph, with the query: *Who is this* [here he gave his name]? And so, at the age of eleven, with the publication of my father's book, I was given the beginnings of the main character of my own first novel.

Financially, the publication of *Gurudeva and other Indian Tales* was a success. A thousand copies were printed and they sold at a dollar, four shillings, high for Trinidad in those days. But the copies went. Of the thousand copies – which at one time seemed so many, occupying so much space in a bedroom – only three or four now survive, in libraries; even my mother has no copy.

Shortly after the publication of *Gurudeva* my father left the *Guardian* for a government job that paid almost twice as well; and during the four or five years he worked for the government he wrote little for himself. He was, at first, 'surveying' rural conditions for a government report. He was, therefore, surveying what he knew, his own background, the background of his early stories. But as a social surveyor compiling facts and figures and tables, no longer a writer concerned with the rituals and manners and what he had seen as the romantic essence of his community, my father was unsettled by what he saw. Out of this unsettlement, and with no thought of publication, he wrote a sketch, 'In the Village', a personal response to the dereliction and

despair by which we were surrounded and which we had all
– even my father, in his early stories – taken for granted.

Later, out of a similar deep emotion, perhaps grief for his
mother, who had died in great, Trinidad poverty in 1942,
he wrote an autobiographical sketch. It was the only piece
of autobiography my father permitted himself, if autobiography can be used of a story which more or less ends with
the birth of the writer. But my father was obsessed by the
circumstances of his birth and the cruelty of his father. I
remember the passion that preceded the writing; I heard
again and again the forty-year-old stories of meanness and of
the expulsion of his pregnant mother from his father's house;
and I remember taking down, at my father's dictation, a page
or two of a version of this sketch.

A version: there were several versions of everything my
father wrote. He always began to write suddenly, after a day
or two of silence. He wrote very slowly; and there always
came a moment when the emotion with which he had
started seemed to have worked itself out and to my surprise
– because I felt I had been landed with his emotion –
something like literary mischief took over.

The autobiographical piece was read, long after it had
been written, to a Port of Spain literary group which
included Edgar Mittelholzer and, I believe, the young
George Lamming. There was objection to the biblical
language and especially to the use of 'ere' for 'before'; but
my father ignored the objection and I, who was very much
under the spell of the story, supported him. 'In the Village'
was printed in a Jamaican magazine edited by Philip
Sherlock.

A reading to a small group, publication in a magazine soon lost to view: writing in Trinidad was an amateur activity, and this was all the encouragement a writer could expect. There were no magazines that paid; there were no established magazines; there was only the *Guardian*. A writer like Alfred Mendes, who in the 1930s had had two novels published by Duckworth in London (one with an introduction by Aldous Huxley and a blurb by Anthony Powell), was said to get as much as twenty dollars, four guineas, for a story in the *Guardian* Sunday supplement; my father only got five dollars, a guinea. My father was a purely local writer, and writers like that ran the risk of ridicule; one of the criticisms of my father's book that I heard at school was that it had been done only for the money.

But attitudes were soon to change. In 1949, the Hogarth Press published Edgar Mittelholzer's novel, *A Morning at the Office*; Mittelholzer had for some time been regarded as another local writer. And then there at last appeared a market. Henry Swanzy was editing *Caribbean Voices* for the BBC Caribbean Service. He had standards and enthusiasm. He took local writing seriously and lifted it above the local. And the BBC paid; not quite at their celebrated guinea-a-minute rate, but sufficiently well – fifty dollars a story, sixty dollars, eighty dollars – to spread a new idea of the value of writing.

Henry Swanzy used two of my father's early stories on *Caribbean Voices*. And from 1950, when he left the government to go back to the *Guardian*, to 1953, when he died, it was for *Caribbean Voices* that my father wrote. In these three years, in circumstances deteriorating month by month – the low *Guardian* pay, debt, a heart attack and subsequent physical incapacity, the hopeless, wounded longing to publish a real book and become in his own eyes a writer – in these three years, with the stimulus of that weekly radio programme from London, my father, I believe, found his voice as a writer, developed his own comic gift, and wrote his best stories.

I didn't participate in the writing of these stories: I didn't watch them grow, or give advice, as I had done with the others. In 1949 I had won a Trinidad government scholarship, and in 1950 I left home to come to England to take up the scholarship. I left my father at the beginning of a story called 'The Engagement'; and it was two years before I read the finished story.

My father wrote me once and sometimes twice a week. His letters, like mine to him, were mainly about money and writing. When Henry Swanzy, in his half-yearly review of *Caribbean Voices*, praised 'The Engagement', my father, who had never been praised like that before, wrote me: 'I am beginning to feel I *could* have been a writer.' But we both felt ourselves in our different ways stalled, he almost at the end of his life, I at the beginning of mine; and our correspondence, as time went on, as he became more broken, and I became more separate from him and Trinidad, more adrift in England, became one of half-despairing mutual encouragement. I had sent him some books by R. K. Narayan, the Indian writer. In March 1952 he wrote: 'You were right about R. K. Narayan. I like his short stories . . . he seems gifted and has made a go of his talent, which in my own case I haven't even spotted.'

In that month he sent me two versions of a story called 'My Uncle Dalloo'. He was uncertain about this story, which he thought long-winded, and wanted me to send what I thought was the better version to Henry Swanzy. I like the story now, for its detail and the drama of its detail; in a small space it creates and peoples a landscape, and the vision is personal. My father hadn't done anything like that before, anything with that amount of historical detail, and I can see the care with which the story is written. I can imagine how those details which he was worried about, and yet was unwilling to lose, were worked over. But at the time – I was nineteen – I took the quality of the vision for granted and saw only the incompleteness of the narrative: my father, working in isolation, had, it might be said, outgrown me.

Henry Swanzy didn't use 'My Uncle Dalloo'. But his judgment of my father's later work was sounder than mine, and he used nearly everything else my father sent him. In June 1953, four months before my father died, Henry Swanzy, at my father's request, asked me to read 'Ramdas and the Cow' for *Caribbean Voices*. The reading fee was four guineas. With the money I bought the Parker pen which I still have and with which I am writing this foreword.

2

Naipaul (or Naipal or Nypal, in earlier transliterations: the transliteration of Hindi names can seldom be exact) was the name of my father's father, birth certificates and other legal requirements have now made it our family name. He was brought to Trinidad as a baby from eastern Uttar Pradesh at some time in the 1880s, as I work it out.

He received no English education but, in the immemorial Hindu way, as though Trinidad was India, he was sent — as a brahmin boy of the Panday clan (or the Parray clan: again, the transliteration is difficult) — to the house of a brahmin to be trained as a pundit. This was what he became; he also, as I have heard, became a small dealer in those things needed for Hindu rituals. He married and had three children; but he died when he was still quite young and his family, unprotected, was soon destitute. My father once told me that at times there wasn't oil for a lamp.

There was some talk, among other branches of the family, of sending the mother and the children back to India; but that plan fell through, and the dependent family was scattered among various relations. My father's elder brother, still only a child, was sent out to work in the fields at fourpence a day; but it was decided that my father, as the youngest of the children, should be educated and perhaps made a pundit, like his father. And that family fracture shows to this day in their descendants. My father's brother, by immense labour, became a small cane-farmer. When I went to see him in 1972, not long before he died, I found him enraged, crying for his childhood and that fourpence a day. My father's sister made two unhappy marriages; she remained, as it were, dazed by Trinidad; until her death in 1972 — more cheerful than her brother, though in a house not her own — she spoke only Hindi and could hardly understand English.

My father received an elementary-school education; he learned English and Hindi. But the attempt to make him a pundit failed. Instead, he began doing odd jobs, attached to the household of a relative (later a millionaire) in that very village of El Dorado which he was to survey more than twenty years later for the government and write about in 'In the Village'.

I do not know how, in such a setting, in those circumstances of dependence and uncertainty, and with no example, the wish to be a writer came to my father. But I feel now, reading the stories after a long time and seeing so clearly (what was once hidden from me) the brahmin standpoint from which they are written, that it might have been the caste-sense, the Hindu reverence for learning and the word, awakened by the beginnings of an English education and a Hindu religious training. In one letter to me he seems to say that he was trying to write when he was fourteen.

He was concerned from the start with Hinduism and the practices of Hinduism. His acquaintance with pundits had given him something of the puritan brahmin prejudice against pundits, professional priests, stage-managers of ritual, as 'tradesmen'. But he had also been given some knowledge of Hindu thought, which he valued; and on this knowledge, evident in the stories, he continued to build throughout his life; as late as 1951 he was writing me ecstatically about Aurobindo's commentaries on the Gita.

The Indian immigrants in Trinidad, and especially the Hindus among them, belonged in the main to the peasantry of the Gangetic plain. They were part of an old and perhaps an ancient India. (It was entrancing to me, when I read Fustel de Coulange's *The Ancient City*, to discover that many of the customs, which with us in Trinidad, even in my childhood, were still like instincts, had survived from the pre-classical world.) This peasantry, transported to Trinidad, hadn't been touched by the great Indian reform movements of the nineteenth century. Reform became an issue only with the arrival of reformist missionaries from India in the 1920s, at a time when in India itself religious reform was merging into political rebellion.

In the great and sometimes violent debates that followed in Trinidad – debates that remained unknown outside the Indian community and are today forgotten by everybody – my father was on the side of reform. The broad satire of the latter part of *Gurudeva* – written in the last year of his life, but not sent to Henry Swanzy – shouldn't be misinterpreted: there my father fights the old battles again, with the passion that in the 1930s had made him spend scarce money on a satirical reform pamphlet, *Religion and the Trinidad East Indians*, one of the books of my childhood, but now lost.

It was on Indian or Hindu topics that my father began writing for the *Trinidad Guardian*, in 1929. The paper had a new editor, Gault MacGowan. He had come from *The Times* and in Trinidad was like a man unleashed. The *Trinidad Guardian*, before MacGowan, was a half-dead colonial newspaper: a large border of advertisements on its front page, a small central patch of closely printed cables. MacGowan's brief was to modernize the *Guardian*. He scrapped that front page. But his taste for drama went beyond the typographical and he began to unsettle some people. Voodoo in backyards, obeah, prisoners escaping from Devil's Island, vampire bats: when the editor of the rival *Port of Spain Gazette* said that MacGowan was killing the tourist trade, MacGowan sued and won. But MacGowan was more than a sensationalist. He was new to Trinidad, discovering Trinidad, and he took nothing for granted. He saw stories everywhere; he could make stories out of nothing; his paper was like a daily celebration of the varied life of the island. But sometimes his wit could run away with him; and the end came when he became involved in a lawsuit with his own employers (which the *Trinidad Guardian*, MacGowan still the editor, reported at length, day after day, so that, in a perfection of the kind of journalism his employers were objecting to, the paper became its own news).

My father had written to MacGowan; and MacGowan, who had been to India and was interested in Indian matters, thought that my father should be encouraged. My father's iconoclastic views, and their journalistic possibilities, must have appealed to him. He became my father's teacher – beginning no doubt with English which, it must be remembered, was for my father an acquired language – and my father never lost his admiration and affection for the man who, as he often said, had taught him how to write. More than twenty years later, in 1951, my father wrote me: 'And as to a writer being hated or liked – I think it's the other way to what you think: a man is doing his work well when people begin *liking* him. I have never forgotten what Gault MacGowan told me years ago: "Write sympathetically"; and this, I suppose, in no way prevents us from writing truthfully, even brightly.'

My father began on the *Guardian* as the freelance contributor of a 'controversial' weekly column. The column – in which I think MacGowan's improving hand can often be detected – was, provocatively, signed 'The Pundit'; and my father remembered the Pundit's words well enough to give blocks of them, years later, to Mr Sohun, the Presbyterian Indian schoolmaster, in the latter part of *Gurudeva*. *Gurudeva* has other echoes of my father's early journalism: Gurudeva's beating up of the drunken old stick-fighter must, I feel, have its origin in the news story my father, now a regular country correspondent for the *Guardian*, wrote in 1930: *Fight Challenge Accepted – Jerningham Junction 'Bully' Badly Injured – Six Men Arrested*. A country brawl dramatized, the personalities brought close to the reader, made more than names in a court report: this was MacGowan's style, and it became my father's.

It was through his journalism on MacGowan's *Guardian* that my father arrived at that vision of the countryside and its people which he later transferred to his stories. And the stories have something of the integrity of the journalism: they are written from within a community and seem to be addressed to that community: a Hindu community essentially, which, because the writer sees it as whole, he can at times make romantic and at other times satirize. There is reformist passion; but even when there is shock there is nothing of the protest – common in early colonial writing – that implies an outside audience; the barbs are all turned inwards. This is part of the distinctiveness of the stories. I stress it because this way of looking, from being my father's, became mine: my father's early stories created my background for me.

But it was a partial vision. A story called 'Panchayat', about a family quarrel, reads like a pastoral romance: the people in that story exist completely within a Hindu culture and recognize no other. The wronged wife does not take her husband to the alien law courts; she calls a panchayat against him. The respected village elders assemble; the wife and the husband state their cases without rancour; everyone is wise and dignified and acknowledges *dharma*, the Hindu right way, the way of piety, the old way. But Trinidad, and not India, is in the background. These people have been transported; old ways and old allegiances are being eroded fast. The setting, which is not described because it is taken for granted, is one of big estates, workers' barracks, huts. It is like the setting of 'In the Village'; but that vision of material and cultural dereliction comes later, and it is some time before it can be accommodated in the stories.

Romance simplified; but it was a way of looking. And it was more than a seeking out of the picturesque; it was also, as I have since grown to understand, a way of concealing personal pain. My father once wrote me: 'I have hardly written a story in which the principal characters have not been members of my own family.' And the wronged wife of 'Panchayat' – as I understood only the other day – was really my father's sister; the details in that story are all true. Her marriage to a Punjabi brahmin (a learned man, who could read Persian, as she told me with pride on her deathbed) was a disaster. My father suffered for her. In the story ritual blurs the pain and, fittingly, all ends well; in life the disaster continued. My father hated his father for his cruelty and meanness; yet when, in his autobiographical sketch, he came to write about his father, he wrote a tale of pure romance, in which again old ritual, lovingly described, can only lead to reconciliation. And my father, in spite of my encouragement, could never take that story any further.

He often spoke of doing an autobiographical novel. Sometimes he said it would be easy; but once he wrote that parts of it would be difficult; he would have trouble selecting the incidents. When in 1952 he sent me 'My Uncle Dalloo' – which he described in another letter, apologetically, as a sketch – he wrote: 'I'd like you to read it carefully, and if you think it good enough, send it to Mr Swanzy, with a note that it's from me; and that it is part of a chapter of a novel I'm doing. Indeed, this is what I aim to do with it. As soon as you can, get working on a novel. Write of things as they are happening now, be realistic, humorous when this comes in pat, but don't make it deliberately so. If you are at a loss for a theme, take me for it. Begin: "He sat before the little table writing down the animal counterparts of all his wife's family. He was very analytical about it. He wanted to be correct; went to work like a scientist. He wrote, 'The She-Fox', then 'The Scorpion'; at the end of five minutes he produced a list which read as follows: . . ." All this is just a jest, but you can really do it.'

But for him it wasn't a jest. Once romance and its simplifications had been left behind, these little impulses of caricature (no more than impulses, and sometimes written out in letters to me), the opposite of MacGowan's 'Write sympathetically', were all he could manage when he came to consider himself and the course of his life. He wrote up the animal-counterparts episode himself (I am sure he was writing it when he wrote that letter to me) and made it part of *Gurudeva*, which had become his fictional hold-all. But even there the episode is sudden and out of character. There is something unresolved about it; the passion is raw and comes out, damagingly, as a piece of gratuitous cruelty on the part of the writer. My father was unhappy about the episode; but he could do no more with it. And this was in the last year of his life, when as a writer – but only looking away from himself – he could acknowledge some of the pain about his family he had once tried to hide, and was able to blend romance and the later vision of dereliction into a purer kind of comedy.

It is my father's sister – once the wronged wife of 'Panchayat', a figure of sorrow in a classical Hindu tableau – who ten years afterwards appears as a road-mender's wife in another story and acts as a kind of comic chorus: the road-mender was the man of lesser caste with whom she went to live after she had separated from her first husband, the Punjabi brahmin. Ramdas of 'Ramdas and the Cow' – the Hindu tormented by the possession of a sixty-dollar cow which turns out to be barren – is my father's elder brother in middle age.

The comedy was for others. My father remained unwilling to look at his own life. All that material, which might have committed him to longer work and a longer view, remained locked up and unused. Certain things can never become material. My father never in his life reached that point of rest from which he could look back at his past. His last years, when he found his voice as a writer, were years of especial distress and anxiety; he was part of the dereliction he wrote about.

My father's elder brother, at the end of his life, was

enraged, as I have said. This sturdy old man, whose life might have been judged a success, was broken by memories of his childhood; self-knowledge had come to him late. My father's own crisis had come at an earlier age; it had been hastened by his journalism. One day in 1934, when he was twenty-eight, five years after he had been writing for the *Guardian*, and some months after Gault MacGowan had left the paper and Trinidad, my father looked in the mirror and thought he couldn't see himself. It was the beginning of a long mental illness that caused him for a time to be unemployed, and as dependent as he had been in his childhood. It was after his recovery that he began writing stories and set himself the goal of the book.

3

Shortly before he died, in 1953, my father assembled all the stories he wanted to keep and sent them to me. He wanted me to get them published as a book. Publication for him, the real book, meant publication in London. But I did not think the stories publishable outside Trinidad, and I did nothing about them.

The stories, especially the early ones, in which I felt I had participated, never ceased to be important to me. But as the years passed – and although I cannibalized his autobiographical sketch for the beginning of one of my own books – my attachment to the stories became sentimental. I valued them less for what they were (or the memory of what they were) than for what, long before, they had given me: a way of looking, an example of labour, a knowledge of the literary process, a sense of the order and special reality (at once simpler and sharper than life) that written words could be seen to create. I thought of them, as I thought of my father's letters, as a private possession.

But the memory of my father's 1943 booklet, *Gurudeva and other Indian Tales*, has never altogether died in Trinidad. Twelve years after his death, my father's stories were remembered by Henry Swanzy in a *New Statesman* issue on Commonwealth writing. In Trinidad itself the attitude to local writing has changed. And my own view has grown longer. I no longer look in the stories for what isn't there; and I see them now as a valuable part of the literature of the region.

They are a unique record of the life of the Indian or Hindu community in Trinidad in the first fifty years of the century. They move from a comprehension of the old India in which the community is at first embedded to an understanding of the colonial Trinidad which defines itself as their background, into which they then merge. To write about a community which has not been written about is not easy. To write about this community was especially difficult; it required unusual knowledge and an unusual breadth of sympathy.

And the writer himself was part of the process of change. This wasn't always clear to me. But I find it remarkable now that a writer, beginning in the old Hindu world, one isolated segment of it, where all the answers had been given and the rituals perfected, and where, apart from religious texts, the only writings known were the old epics of the Ramayana and the Mahabharat; leaving that to enter a new world and a new language; using simple, easily detectable models – Pearl Buck, O. Henry; I find it remarkable that such a writer, working always in isolation, should have gone so far. I don't think my father read Gogol; but these stories, at their best, have something of the quality of the Ukrainian stories Gogol wrote when he was a very young man. There is the same eye that lingers lovingly over what might at first seem nondescript. Landscape, dwellings, people: there is the same assembling of sharp detail. The drama lies in that; when what has been relished is recorded and fixed, the story is over.

Gogol at the beginning of his writing life, my father at the end of his: even if the comparison is just, it can mislead. After his young man's comedy and satire, after the discovery and exercise of his talent, Gogol had Russia to fall back on and claim. It was the other way with my father. From a vision of a whole Hindu society he moved, through reformist passion, which was an expression of his brahmin confidence, to a vision of disorder and destitution, of which he discovered himself to be part. At the end he had nothing to claim; it was out of this that he created comedy.

The process is illustrated by *Gurudeva*. This story isn't satisfactory, especially in some of its later sections; and my father knew it. Part of the trouble is that the story was written in two stages. The early sections, which were written in 1941–2, tell of the beginnings of a village strongman. The character (based, remotely, on someone who had married into my mother's family but had then been expelled from it, the mention of his name forbidden) is not as negligible as he might appear now. He belongs to the early 1930s and, in those days of restricted franchise, he might have developed (as the original threatened to develop) into a district politician. Although in the story he is simplified, and his idea of manhood ridiculed as thuggery and a perversion of the caste instinct, Gurudeva is felt to be a figure. And in its selection of strong, brief incidents, its gradual peopling of an apparently self-contained Indian countryside (other communities are far away), this part of the story is like the beginning of a rural epic.

Ten years later, when my father returned to the story (and brought Gurudeva back from jail, where in 1942 he had sent him), the epic tone couldn't be sustained. Gurudeva's Indian world was not as stable as Gurudeva, or the writer, thought. The society had been undermined; its values had to compete with other values; the world outside the village could no longer be denied. As seen in 1950–2, Gurudeva, the caste bully of the 1930s, becomes an easy target. Too easy: the irony and awe with which he had been handled in the first part of the story turns to broad satire, and the satire defeats itself.

Mr Sohun the schoolmaster, the Presbyterian convert, holds himself up, and is held up by the writer, as a rational man, freed from Hindu prejudice and obscurantism. But Mr Sohun, whose words in the 1930s might have seemed wise, is himself now seen more clearly. It is hinted – he hints himself: my father makes him talk too much – that he is of low caste. His Presbyterianism is more than an escape from this: it is, as Gurudeva says with sly compassion, Mr Sohun's bread and butter, a condition of his employment as a teacher in the Canadian Mission school. Mr Sohun's son has the un-

Indian name of Ellway. But the boy so defiantly named doesn't seem to have done much or to have much to do. When Gurudeva calls, Ellway is at home, noisily knocking up fowl-coops: the detail sticks out.

In fact, the erosion of the old society has exposed Mr Sohun, and the writer, as much as Gurudeva. The writer senses this; his attitude to Gurudeva changes. The story jumps from the 1930s to the late 1940s. Gurudeva, no longer a caste bully and a threat, becomes a figure of comedy; and, curiously, his stature grows. He is written into the story of 'Ramdas and the Cow' (originally an independent story); turning satirist himself, he writes down the animal counterparts of his wife's family and begins to approximate to his creator; at the end, abandoned by wife and girl friend and left alone, he is a kind of brahmin, an upholder of what remains of old values, but powerless. He has travelled the way of his baffled creator.

Writers need a source of strength other than that which they find in their talent. Literary talent doesn't exist by itself; it feeds on a society and depends for its development on the nature of that society. What is true of my father is true of other writers of the region. The writer begins with his talent, finds confidence in his talent, but then discovers that it isn't enough, that, in a society as deformed as ours, by the exercise of his talent he has set himself adrift.

★

4

I have not attempted to change the idiosyncrasies of my father's English; I have corrected only one or two obvious errors. In the later stories (partly because he was writing for the radio) he wrote phonetic dialogue. Phonetic dialogue – apart from its inevitable absurdities: *eggszactly* for 'exactly', *w'at* for 'what' – falsifies the pace of speech, sets up false associations, is meaningless to people who don't know the idiom and unnecessary to those who do. The rhythm of broken language is sufficiently indicated by the construction of a sentence. I have toned down this phonetic dialogue, modelling myself on my father's more instinctive and subtle rendering of speech in *Gurudeva and other Indian Tales*; like my father in that early booklet, I have not aimed at uniformity.

My father dedicated his stories to me. But the style of publication has changed; and I would like to extend this dedication to the two men who stand at the beginning and end of my father's writing career: to Gault MacGowan, to whom I know my father wanted to dedicate *Gurudeva and other Indian Tales* in 1943; and to Henry Swanzy.

June 1975   V. S. NAIPAUL

A School Inspection

Gurudeva was only fourteen years old when he was taken away from the Mission School in the village in order to be married. He made no objections, and even if he had, it is doubtful whether Jaimungal, his father, would have let him off lightly. It is just possible that he would have put him out of the house as a *pukka badmash*, or at least given him a sound beating.

Old Jaimungal was regarded by everybody in the village as a staunch Hindu, and as such he could not of course tolerate marrying a son who had already grown a moustache. More-over, he was sure – though he could not say exactly why, for he was not one who could read and write well enough to understand the subtleties of the Shastras – he was sure that marrying a son after that son had already crossed his teens was an odiously un-Hindu affair. And then, too, a *doolaha* or bridegroom looked so much the more picturesque in his flowing wedding gown and tall scintillating crown if his face behind the low-hanging tassels of the crown – colloqui-ally called a wedding hat – was a boyish face; not one marred by whiskers. Otherwise even the most telling of regalias served only to emphasize the marrying one's hardness of features. A state of things compatible only with low-caste Hindus.

Gurudeva was actually in school giving up his lesson on tenses with a semicircle of boys at the headteacher's desk, when his father, accompanied by a heavy little man, came to show him off.

The little man was a portly person in dusty, unlaced shoes. He had a white skull-cap on his head and, unlike Jaimungal, who wore trousers and shirt, was clad in dhoti and *koortah*. His broad forehead was decorated with three horizontal lines of white sandal paste, and he carried a parasol on the crook of one arm. His features were rather vague, but he seemed well-fed and prosperous. Once he shifted the tight-fitting skull-cap and you saw that his hair was partly black and partly grey. He could not have been more than forty-five, or fifty, perhaps.

Immediately Gurudeva saw them he guessed the purpose of the visit. The knowledge made him partly proud and partly shy; but he tried to behave as though he had not seen them.

'Schoolmaster,' Jaimungal called, a shade obsequiously, 'good evening!' He took off his faded felt hat, and you saw that his hair too was streaked with grey. He was built on the large side and was tall and long-limbed.

Mr Sohun came up and shook hands cordially with both persons. He was a dapper little man.

'This is Pundit Sookhlal,' Jaimungal said, indicating his portly companion. 'He come to have a look at the boy, Schoolmaster.'

Pundit Sookhlal bowed, shifted the parasol from the one arm to the other.

'You see, Schoolmaster,' Jaimungal explained in an under-tone, 'I think I goin' to get the boy married.'

Mr Sohun lifted his eyebrows.

'You know, Schoolmaster, how boys get out of hand these days?'

Mr Sohun was taken aback. He pursed his lips and threw out his chest. He had a broad chest.

'It's your affair, of course,' he said; 'but the boy is only in the third standard. Besides, he is absurdly young for marrying. I thought you would give at least this son of yours a chance. You are not a poor man, you know. You are one of the biggest cane-farmers this side of the colony, and you can afford giving the boy a good education – possibly a profession.'

Old man Jaimungal gave a half deprecating, half patroniz-ing smile. It was a smile, in fact, that plainly told Mr Sohun that he didn't know better. 'This,' thought the old man, 'is what comes of sending one's children to school. Always they want you to conform to practices outside your religion.'

He waved the reminder with a short flourish of his hand. 'That is orright, Schoolmaster,' he said. 'He know 'nough. He could read. He could write a letter. He could even write a receipt. What mo' he want?'

Mr Sohun saw the futility of argument. He couldn't possibly put right all the wrong things in the world, but he could at least give a warning and wash his hands of the business.

'Very well, Jaimungal. Do as you please.' He bowed shortly and returned to his class. 'Go,' he said to Gurudeva; 'your father wants you.' And, as the boy turned to leave the class, Mr Sohun grinned and added, in a somewhat quizzical tone, 'Wedding for you, boy!'

There was a titter, and all the boys looked up perkily. Gurudeva wilted with shame. Then he went away and stood dutifully before his father. He did not look at the other man. He knew what the other man had come for and he was shy to look into his eyes.

'This is the boy, Punditji,' Gurudeva heard his father say proudly. 'He grow big for he age.'

Pundit Sookhlal looked the lad up and down most appraisingly and seemed to melt with pleasure. He patted Gurudeva lightly and affectionately on the shoulder. 'He will do,' he said in Hindi. 'He is just the match for my Ratni.'

A fortnight later Gurudeva was a married 'man'.

Gurudeva as Husband

Gurudeva himself could not say whether he loved or hated Ratni. She was twelve years old, small and plump and pretty with a full brown face. Her eyes were large and dark, her movement slow, and there was something in her attitude that suggested the significant casualness of the martyr. She hardly spoke and seldom smiled, and it was difficult to say when she had last laughed. Gurudeva himself would not let her laugh, because, he said, that was bad manners in a newly married girl; and if she sometimes forgot and did laugh out, he promptly silenced her with a look, if not with a slap. Indeed, the time came when Ratni often found herself in the very puzzling position of not knowing which was the worse – to laugh or to cry. If she laughed, there was Gurudeva to crush her with a glance or stun her with a slap; if she cried, Jhulani, her mother-in-law, let her know, in no mean tone, that she was a most sulky and trying person – the embodiment of ill-omen in the house.

But it was not always thus. When she first came everybody liked her – very much. Almost to suffocation. She was decidedly the pet of the house. They called her *doolahin*, bride, which was in itself a pet name. She reigned a queen, and like a queen she could do no wrong; and if she did happen on anything that seemed not right, everybody, but especially Jhulani, glorified the blunder. It was looked upon as the harmless, innocent prank of a child; something to be amused at, something to enjoy. Jhulani gave every evidence that she was both proud and fond of Ratni. Oh yes, Ratni herself could say that. Jhulani would put Ratni right in front of her, undo her hair and pick out every nit and every louse. And then she would say, 'Now, *doolahin*, come and pick *my* head.'

All very motherly, to be sure.

But the thing had not lasted. Three months – and she was no longer a novelty. She was hated. Everybody hated her – even the old man, the old man who used to bring her 'sweeties' every so often. How it started – this business of hate and apathy against her – she could not say. It was gradual, like the subtle, insidious growth of a disease. The little blunders that had hitherto called forth smiles and gay laughter were now looked upon as wilful wickedness ... Now the rice was too soft-boiled; now the dahl had too much salt; now the *roti* was burnt; now she had stood before old Jaimungal with her *orhani*, veil, off her head ... There was no end to complaints.

Nevertheless, Ratni's coming in the house brought Gurudeva a definite prestige, and, automatically enough, he found himself wanting to behave as a man. He was suddenly ponderously precocious. He discarded his short trousers for long ones and tried by innuendoes as well as by a variety of subtle and tangible ways to impress his wife that he was not one to be trifled with; that, in fact, he was his own man –

her man at any rate – and that, in virtue of it, he could beat her with impunity whenever he chose to do so. Which was often.

Gurudeva became a prodigy at quarrelling – especially with Ratni. As the conjurer produces a florin apparently from nowhere, in some such manner he would evolve a quarrel out of nothing. She might cast a timid glance at him, and he would say in a voice as though he had seen a *mapepire* snake, 'Now, why the hell you lookin' at me like that for?' And she would answer, 'Who lookin' at you? Me? Well, an' you must be lookin' at me, too.' And that, Gurudeva would find, was 'too much back-answer'; and he would right away busy himself on her with fist or foot, or with almost anything he could catch hold of.

Gurudeva was cruel, to be sure; but in his cruelty there was no malice and little, if any, anger. Once he caught, back of the house, a stray puppy sucking hen's eggs in a clump of bush. Suddenly he pounced upon the dog and grabbed it by the hind leg, and called out to Ratni to bring him a bag; and when she brought it he put the puppy in it and gathered the ends and lifted the bag with the dog in it. Then, with every step that he took forward, he bumped the bag on the ground; and every time that the creature yelped with the thud, Gurudeva laughed outright in sheer delight. But somehow one corner of the bag slipped down his fingers and out dashed the puppy.

'You bugger!' he exclaimed. 'You run, eh?'

He was not angry. He was just having a good joke. And, had the puppy not escaped, he would have put a steaming egg into its mouth. Not because he hated the creature; but just to break its habit of stealing eggs.

So, too, he beat Ratni; not from any overwhelming surge of anger, nor from any conscious wickedness, but because the privilege and prerogative of beating her was his, by virtue of his being her husband. He was not doing anything shameful. He was only beating his wife. It would be a fine world if a man could not beat his own wife!

And Ratni knew this, too, young as she was, and bore up under her travails without complaint and without murmur, as any good wife was expected to do. And her father and mother knew this likewise and were often sorrowful about the whole rotten affair, but would hardly put in a word of protest, old and knowing as they were.

3

The Beating of Ratni

It was in the fifth year of her marriage, when she was nearly seventeen, that Ratni got her worst mauling. That day Gurudeva was really angry. Ratni was in the kitchen, preparing the midday food, when he came rushing in.

'Ei!' he called. 'What about me food?' He jammed his hands against his waist, pressed his teeth on his lower lip and waited ominously for answer.

Ratni grew pale. She sensed trouble. She had not yet finished cooking the midday food.

'Come on, I waitin'!' thundered Gurudeva.

Long spoon in hand, Ratni turned from the pot and faced him, trembling in every limb. She said:

'I – I was washing clothes today. There was plenty to wash. I will give you food jus' now ... Two minute ... The *bharth* finish, the dahl finish too; the *bhaji* cookin'.'

'*Bhaji*! What *bhaji*?' roared Gurudeva.

'Pumpkin vine wid sal'fish.'

'Pumpkin vine! Who tell you to cook pumpkin vine?'

'But you always eat it. I thought ...'

'Back-answer, eh!' spluttered Gurudeva. 'I will show you.'

And he pounced upon her, even as he had pounced upon

the puppy, and bundled her out into the yard. Artfully he entwined her long hair around his fists and dragged her in a circle over the rough ground as though she were a sack of potatoes. And when she neither wailed nor wept, he disengaged his hands from her hair and cuffed her and kicked her fanatically. His large, taut neck grew tauter, and his dark face darker. He foamed at the mouth. He was terrifying . . .

'You wouldn't cry, eh? You playing you could take blows . . . Well, take blows . . . ' And he chucked her off and undid his harness-leather belt and flogged her and flogged her with it till the belt became too short for further use, and she, instead of howling with mortal pain, suddenly laughed out long and loudly, like a creature gone stark mad; and in that hard, mad gladness she shouted out, 'Beat me today, kill me and bury me!'

Then he was suddenly alarmed at her frenzy, and not letting her know he was alarmed, he left her.

In a heap, there she sprawled on the ground, inert as though dead. And there it was that Mira and Dhira, her elder sisters-in-law, found her, when they returned from the ricelands, drenched and dripping, two hours later. Trembling with the cold as much as because of what had been done to Ratni, they stooped either side of her and held her under the armpits and helped to get her on her feet. Groaning and sagging, Ratni stood up, and leaning against their shoulders, allowed herself to be carried and put upon her *khatiah*, the bed of hempen string, in the little room back of the house, which was hers and Gurudeva's.

Then, still in their wet clothes, Mira and Dhira went down the track that led to the saffron patch in the cane-field.

They brought saffron. Mira set to grinding the saffron into a paste with coconut oil on the stone slab used for grinding massala; while Dhira tore up into strips an old *orhani* for bandage. Then together they laid the saffron paste thick upon the body of Ratni – on all the parts of her body that were blue and black and bruised with the kicking and cuffing and belting of Gurudeva.

And a poignant sorrow assailed Mira and Dhira as they ministered unto the hapless Ratni, and they wept till the tears flooded their eyes too much and they quickly brushed them away so as to see where and how to apply the healing paste.

And thus they felt because they knew that such was their lot as well, and they wondered in a vague, resigned sort of way why the Deity had allowed them to be born at all. For they had ever heard it taught by their fathers, by the elders of the village, as well as by the pundits who often read the *Ramayana* on evenings, that the husband was to the wife God, lord and master – all in one – and that a woman's highest virtue lay in her absolute submission to her husband's will – be that will of whatever complexion.

'But you see,' Dhira told Mira in Hindi, 'it is all a very one-sided operation. They want us all to be like Sita – that is, to try as far as possible to be like her; but on the other hand, *they* are far from being like Rama, the incarnation of the great God Vishnu himself. They do not even try. It is not fair. But wipe your tears, little sister. It is our karma.'

And in the days that followed the healing of Ratni, Gurudeva hardly spoke to anybody in the house, but took his food from one or the other of his sisters-in-law in the

morning and ate it squatting on the floor, silently and
sullenly. Then he would leave the house, returning at the
midday hour; and he would eat and leave the house once
more and would not return till late evening. He would then
eat again and go to sleep in the hammock in the long, open
gallery, away from Ratni, sullen and morose as ever.

On the third evening his father came to him by the
hammock. Quietly, almost timidly, in a tone half patronizing,
half admonitory, the old man said to him in Hindi:

'Son, it is not good to be like this. Be not cast down.
What is to be will be.'

And Gurudeva looked up quickly and questioningly, as
though the old man should have expressed a less silly thought,
and rapped out in Hindi:

'Well, I have no patience with her. She is rude and crude
and gives me back-answers.'

The old man nodded understandingly and put one hand
on the shoulder of his son and said sympathetically:

'I know that. But she is only a woman and will be ever
foolish, no matter what you do; but *you* must keep your
temper, for you can read and write, and know good from
bad . . . But she – well, to her letters are like dirt.'

Phulmati, Ratni's mother, was turning paddy on a bagspread
in the sun out in the yard when Jokhoo – tramp, story-teller,
and matrimonial matchmaker – brought news of the beating
of Ratni.

Wiping the sweat off his face with the hanging bit of his

dingy turban – for it was midday and pelting hot – Jokhoo said:

'And thoroughly has Gurudeva done her in this time. With kick and cuff and belt he has laid her low. Aho! Aho!' And the old man slumped down against the earth wall and sighed as though it was he who had been beaten.

Phulmati stopped turning the paddy. 'They will kill my child,' she said with conviction. 'I know they will. The hard-hearts! Shame they have not got to beat a young girl like that!'

And she went down on her haunches and smote her forehead resoundingly with her palms and fell to weeping. Then, recollecting herself, she quickly dashed away her tears with a corner of her *orhani*, and said bravely and understand-ingly, 'Well, it is her karma; I gave her birth, but for her karma I was not responsible.'

'Now you are talking sense, woman,' said Pundit Sookhlal. One dhoti-clad leg crossed upon the other, he sat naked-back on the bamboo bench in the open trash-covered hut. He was trying to coax a smoke from a sweaty *cheelum*, an Indian smoking-pipe, which would not respond.

'Ari! Ari!' he said. 'The more I ponder over the sufferings of Ratni, the clearer I see – as in a mirror – that whatever befalls the girl – whether of woe or weal – it is neither the doings of Gurudeva, nor mine, nor anybody else's, but Ratni's herself. She is simply reaping what she had sown in her previous life; just as how I and you, and Jokhoo here, are each reaping whatever we had sown. Only a fool will try to stop the workings of karma.'

Pundit Sookhlal thoughtfully fingered the bowl of his

cheelum. 'Yet, against all the dark, menacing clouds of her life,' he said, 'I see one gleaming thing that makes me almost happy – certainly proud: it is fine how Ratni is putting up with everything. Thank God for that. It says a lot for the exemplary upbringing I have bequeathed her.'

And the pundit once more drew heroically at the *cheelum*, which now seemed dead. 'Bring me another lump of fire,' he said. 'This stupid *cheelum* has gone cold again.'

4

The Making of a Bad-John

Gurudeva was ambitious. From boyhood he was obsessed with a craving for fame. Had other things been equal he might at least have risen to the distinction of a legislator; he might have been a doctor or a lawyer or an electrical engineer; for his father was wealthy as well as indulgent. But Gurudeva remained where we find him, not only because he was divorced from the Mission School when he had gone no further than the third standard, but also because, as in boyhood, so in later life, he ever lacked a sense of selection and went on mistaking notoriety for fame.

Now, at twenty-two, his whole ambition was to be noticed. It was not enough that he had made his presence felt and feared in the house. It was not enough that his father, his mother, his two elder brothers and their wives stood in awe of him. He wanted to be looked upon with awe by the whole village. He hankered to be popular, but to be popular in a spectacular way. He wanted people to point at him and whisper, 'See that fellow going there? He is Gurudeva, the bad-John!'

This fancy of Gurudeva was born mainly of the stories that old Jaimungal often told on evenings of the dare-devil exploits of dead and gone bad-Johns. He would squat out in the open gallery, and the people living near his house – the best and biggest in the village, since it was roofed with galvanized iron and floored with board and had jalousies in the doors and windows and was painted in red and blue and yellow – the neighbours would come and squat before him with their dhoti-clad haunches on the floor and their knees going up to their chins; and they would listen entranced to the stories he told.

And among them the most entranced listener would be Gurudeva.

'Those were the days!' the old man would say exultantly. 'There was that fellow Khardukhan, for instance. Well, he was a great one for a fighter! Could he play the *gatka*? On Hosey Day especially he broke many heads. He was born to fight. Policemen! He would break their heads too. Jail! He used to say that jail was not made for dogs. There was none to touch him. On Hosey Day, when all the competing hoseys met at the junction before Lee Tung's long provision shop, he would throw his stick into the ring and bravely give out his challenge. "Ya, Hassan! Any man!" Ha! But few dared to tilt stick with Khardukhan. And if any did – well, that one was sure to retire with a broken head.

'Blood. That was what Khardukhan's stick drew.'

And the old man would pause significantly and say in a low tone, 'You see, his stick was mounted!' (With the rebellious spirit of a volatile Spaniard.) A far-away look would steal into his eyes . . . 'And so was Nanna. Nanna now . . . ' And he would reel forth from the recesses of his memory the amazing exploits of another hero, and of yet another, until the night would be far gone, and the doleful cry of the poor-me-one, otherwise the zombie-bird, the croaking choruses of frogs, the menacing chant of the mosquitoes, and the midnight crowing of cocks would make him yawn and say it was time to sleep.

And hearing these tales, Gurudeva's blood boiled within him, and he vowed to become a bad-John too.

5

Bhakhiranji

It should be said for Gurudeva that once a fancy possessed his mind, he set about translating it into action for all he was worth. He told no one of this new consuming ambition of his. It was too sacred for words; but he absented himself more and more from the rice-lands, leaving his share of the work to his two brothers, Ramnath and Makhan, and their wives.

Making sticks for fighting purposes became his hobby. He spared himself no pains making them. He would take himself into the high woods up in Chickland, three miles away, and cut the pouis that flourished abundantly on the high lands, and gathering them into a bundle, he would tote them home.

Out in the yard he would make a blazing fire of dry leaves and bake the sticks in it and beat the barks off them on the ground. Then he would cut each stick into the desired length – from ground level to his lower ribs – and then with cutlass, with broken bottles with razor-sharp edges, and finally with sandpaper, he would impart to each stick the smoothness and uniformity of a ruler. Then he would go to the giant bamboo clump near by and bring forth a length of bamboo, stout and ripe and roomy in its hollowness, and an inch or two longer than his stick; and he would punch out all the compartments but the last, and order Ratni to make enough oil from coconuts and fill the bamboo vessel with it to the very top.

It would be done.

Into the bamboo he would immerse as many of his precious sticks as it could hold. Then he would stand the vessel in a corner of his room and would not bring out the sticks from it till ten days or a fortnight, when he would let off a whoop of joy. For the sticks would be found to have taken on a rich brown colour and almost twice the weight they had before their protracted bath.

And Gurudeva, in an ecstasy of pleasure, would in turn hold each stick and bring the ends forward until the stick formed a semicircle; and though he would not risk making the ends actually meet, for fear the stick would break, he would boast he could do it.

'It goin' take blows in a fight without breaking anyway,' he told his father on one occasion. 'For it would limber and not break or let off splinters.'

And the old man shook his head and marvelled at the wisdom and industry of the youth.

Gurudeva loved his sticks. They were the joy of his heart. He had them standing in a row against the wall at the head of his *khatiah*; and, deep in the night, in the light of the unshaded oil-lamp, he would find himself wide awake and flat on his belly. Chin in cupped hands, he would contemplate his sticks with the intensity of a miser gloating over his treasure.

And then Gurudeva's joy would desert him and he would turn on his back and begin to worry. 'There is no sense in having sticks without having them mounted,' he thought. 'An' it is jus' as foolish to want to become a bad-John without bein' a able stickman.'

He knew no one who mounted sticks and he knew not even the rudiments of the art of the *gatka* or duel with sticks. He sought out his father one morning and begged him to help him out of his difficulties. 'Tell me, Bap,' he begged, 'wey I can find a good stick-mounter? I mean somebody who really know the job.'

The old man was squatting on his heels out in the yard, scraping his tongue with a split bit of twig as part of the morning ablutions. A glad gleam lit his eyes. His little sparrow was getting to be a hawk. He finished scraping his tongue, and said:

'A mounter? Why, there is no better man than Bhakhiran.' Jaimungal spoke in Hindi. 'He is old and shaky now, but he still retains his powers. Oh, yes. You will find him in his tapia hut in the next village.'

Gurudeva beamed. First he would see to getting his sticks mounted, then he would see about practising the *gatka*.

It didn't take Gurudeva long to locate Bhakhiran's hut. An old woman, possibly Bhakhiran's wife, sat on her haunches, scouring brass plates under a mango tree in the yard back of the hut. A big girl, possibly Bhakhiran's daughter, came in, hot and sweaty, with a bundle of cow's fodder on her head. She threw down the bundle upon a *matchan* next to a palm-thatched pen, wiped the sweat off

40

her face duck-fashion against her shoulder, and, without a word, went back the way she had come.

Gurudeva, a burning cigarette between his fingers, gave a low cough. It was a discreet and respectful cough which conveyed at the same time a weighty salutation.

The crone, swathed in faded voluminous skirt and *jhoolah*, or bodice, craned her neck and saw Gurudeva. Interest lit her eyes.

'You want something?' she asked. Her words were mongrel Hindi, a sort of patois Hindi which, spoken elsewhere but in Trinidad, would be unmeaning gibberish.

Gurudeva said: 'Yes, yes. I want to see Bhakhiranji. It is important.'

'Wait a little.'

The old woman stood up and waddled into the hut. 'There is a man here. He says he wants to see you.'

She stood in the doorway and waited. From within came a gurgle, a croaking and then a voice that sounded like the breaking of a calabash. The old woman turned to Gurudeva.

'You may come in,' she said, and returned to her work.

Gurudeva was shocked. He found himself looking down, as it were, not so much at a man as at a huge morocoy. For Bhakhiranji was a crumpled, wheezy, sagging old man – more sick than old – and it seemed to Gurudeva that the derelict of a man did not have enough backbone to enable him to sit up.

He was all in a recumbent heap on a bed of stripped *bois-canot* overlaid with dry tapia grass and sugar-bags and flour-sacks. Only his head moved now and then, in the manner of a morocoy's.

41

His thin, merino-clad belly was pressing on his legs as on pillows, and his chin – a gnarled thing – was resting on one knee. His feet were drawn in under his lean shanks and he wore a length of mildewed, dirt-sodden cotton for dhoti, which was not so much a cover as an apology for one. Its scantiness, thinness and dirt made it an offence. His hair, mouse-grey, was thin and sparse. His eyes, large and bleary, were sunken in their sockets. His collar-bones suggested rusty iron rings held under taut elastic. His whole attitude was one long cry.

Gurudeva knew not what to do. He felt it would be brutal to burden the old man with the business he had come to have with him. And then, as though someone else were speaking for him, he heard himself saying in Hindi:

'Bhakhiranji, how are you? I hope you are feeling better.'

The old man croaked and jerked his head up morocoy-like and looked at him. The mounter of sticks made an effort to speak, but no words came; only a surge of racking cough. The convulsions held for about thirty seconds, but to Gurudeva those thirty seconds seemed more like thirty minutes. When the coughing subsided, he said:

'Bhakhiranji, I have come to you on a very important business.'

Bhakhiranji asked: 'First, who may you be? I cannot say I have known you before. You see, I have been tied down to this bed for years.'

'Oh, I am Gurudeva, son of Jaimungal.'

The old man seemed vastly relieved. 'Oh, sit down. There is the box,' he said.

Gurudeva sat down.

'I knew your father,' gurgled the old man. 'He was somewhat of a *gatka*-man in his time. But you do not know about that. You were too small; or maybe you were not yet born.'

'It is about stick-playing that I have come to you, Bhakhiranji. I want you to mount my sticks.'

Bhakhiranji was visited by another bout of coughing, and when the paroxysm was over, he asked: 'Can you play the *gatka*?

'Not yet, but I will learn it. I will learn it, Bhakhiranji.'

The old man said: 'Yes, yes; to be sure you will. You have long limbs that will make for fine reaches. But you see, it is no use having mounted sticks without knowing the art of the *gatka*. Your stick will draw blood, to be sure; but you have to fend too. No stick will fend for you.'

Gurudeva wondered at the wisdom of the man.

'Bring your stick tomorrow,' said Bhakhiranji. 'I will mount it for you. Just because you are Jaimungal's son. It will cost you a cock – a big cock; a quart of rum – puncheon rum; some tobacco – good tobacco. And – well, yes – five dollars for labour. Just five dollars; because you are Jaimungal's son.'

He had another bout of coughing and when it gave him a chance, he said: 'That is all. But listen! Do not let anyone touch the mounted stick. It will want to draw blood. 'Panish, you know! All right. Bring your stick tomorrow – along with the material.'

Gurudeva was impressed – tremendously impressed. 'I will, I will,' he said ecstatically.

And he did.

In time Gurudeva had as many as half a dozen sticks mounted by the dare-devil spirit of Bhakhiranji's gore-thirsty Spaniard. And once, when Ratni at an unguarded moment observed that he had but two hands, and what would he do with so many sticks, Gurudeva promptly silenced her with a slap. 'Mind you' own business,' he said. 'Don' put goat-mouth.'

Every time he brought home a newly mounted stick he would warn Ratni in a hushed, mysterious tone, 'Take care now! Don' touch this stick. It is mounted. It will want to draw blood every time you touch it.'

And Ratni would open her large eyes larger yet, and let awe shine forth from them, but would not say a word again, lest she say the wrong thing.

It was not long before Gurudeva's father and his mother, as well as his brothers and their wives and – mysteriously enough – almost everybody in the village, knew that Gurudeva was a man who kept mounted sticks; and they respected and feared him for that as much as they respected and feared the sticks themselves.

Old Jaimungal especially looked up to Gurudeva at this time with pride. Gurudeva was a Brahmin by birth and a Kshatriya by valour. Like Arjuna, the renowned warrior prince of yore! As far as he knew – and he knew a lot – every real bad-John in Trinidad was the son of a Kshatriya, the princely and soldier caste in the Hindu social hierarchy. Well, it was in his blood. But to have the qualities of a Brahmin and those of a Kshatriya, too – well, that was a unique combination.

And when Gurudeva sought out an *oustard* or veteran

stickman and at his guidance began practising on evenings at *gatka*, which they play at Hosey time; and at creole stick, which they play at Carnival time and in fighting mêlées generally, old Jaimungal positively began to boast. He did not give a jot that Gurudeva was contemptuous of all real work. Wasn't he the famed one in the family? If his elder brothers bothered him any too much about doing his share of the work in rice-land or cane-field, Guru was just the man to beat *them*, too, and put them in their place. But no; he must not let that happen. People would laugh.

And Gurudeva did not waste time. He rallied together most of the young fellows in the village and announced the formation of a *gatka* band. The meeting took place on the big bridge that spanned the river half a mile away from Gurudeva's house. The fellows sat on the whitewashed concrete rails with their legs dangling before them. It was late evening, but an argent moon gave forth all the light that was necessary for the occasion. Dinnoo was there, and Jairam and Ramlal and Birbal; and Hansraj, the veteran *gatka*-man, whom everybody called *Oustard*, which was the same thing like calling him the champion.

'The thing is,' Gurudeva said, speaking English now, 'that this is a dam slack village. Why, we ain't doing one thing for the name of the place. Better we was all in frocks instead of in pants.'

'It is the struth,' agreed Dinnoo, who was Gurudeva's best supporter. 'It is a shame and something mus' be done about it.'

The *Oustard* put in: 'You boys mus' form up a *gatka* band.

That is what you have to do. Hosey is two months off an' you can show you'self then.'

'Exactly!' said Gurudeva. 'What you sayin', boys? *Oustard* here can teach we. Each of we can give 'im a shillin' in the fortnight. Twelve of we will make him get twelve shillings. And we will throw up an' buy we own pitchoil for flambeau. Come on, what you sayin'?'

'We ain't sayin' nothing,' said Jairam, who already knew some *gatka*. 'We ain't sayin' no.'

'I agree too,' Ramlal added.

'And I ain't sayin' no. We all agree. Is a *gatka* band we going to have.' This was Dinnoo, son of Birbal the thatcher.

The motion was adopted unanimously, and – let it be said – enthusiastically. It was planned that they must each be proficient to 'breaks' for himself on Hosey Day, when opposing *gatka*-men would meet in combat before Lee Tung's rumshop at the three-roads junction.

They practised assiduously and with gusto, but none more so than Gurudeva. An hour or so before practice time – for that took place in flambeau light – Gurudeva would take his stick and go and take his stand by the kerbstone at the crossroads. He would be hatless and he would contrive to let his hair stand wild and rebellious. He wanted to look reckless and bad. His short-sleeved shirt would be open all down his chest, and he would stand against the kerbstone with folded arms, his stick held conspicuously down one closed fist. Tall he had grown now and his shoulders had broadened and his chest become heavier and hairier; and he was quite aware of all this and let the people take notice.

Keeping at that tense pose, he would not smile. Not he!

His whole attitude told the passer-by: 'You see me, I am not joking. Just say something funny and you will see!'

But like the monkey that is said to know instinctively which branch to swing upon, Gurudeva knew whom to trouble. He never provoked a real fighter or anyone who at all looked like a fighter. He would consort with such. He knew his limitations. He knew that in spite of his best efforts he could not very well strike and parry without sustaining blows. He lacked the sixth sense, the ingenuity, the nimble-ness — and, above all, the innate recklessness that went to make the true bad-John and the expert *gatka*-man.

But he had tact, and it is to his credit that from the outset he became the leader of the village bad-John clique. His tallness and carriage invested him with a character and individuality that served him well. He was the leader. He brought about all the fights — at weddings, at Hosey time, at Carnival, on pay-day Saturdays — but in almost every case the others did the spade work.

Sometimes their exploits had their sequels in the police court, but Gurudeva would let everybody see that he didn't care a button. Once he went up to his father and said:

'Bap, the whole thing comin' out in court. Jairam, Ramlal, Dinnoo, meself — all of we is in it. But, Bap, don' pay for me. I will take jail for it. I is a man!'

And old Jaimungal felt great and puffed out his chest in pride. In the end he paid not only for Gurudeva, but for all his colleagues involved in the fracas.

And that was one reason — in fact it was *the* reason — why Gurudeva remained the leader of the village bad men.

6

Hosey!

Gurudeva never became a good stickman. He even decided to build a hosey, but this he did mainly to keep up the spirits of the members of his clique. To his father, however, he confided that he was building a hosey because he had gone and made a vow to Hassan to do so. The old man, without questioning him, understood. Naturally, Gurudeva wanted to become the father of a man-child. So he had vowed that he would build hoseys in memory of Hassan and Hussein for five consecutive years.

'You will have to offer them a cock too,' said the old man. 'And *maleeda* – sweetmeat. Go ahead, boy; try you' luck.'

Gurudeva had no idea as to the real significance of Hosey. In some vague way – mainly from the plaintive songs that the women sang during Hosey days – he gathered that it had something to do with two brothers, Hassan and Hussein. Some said that they were the adopted grandsons of Mohammed the prophet. He didn't know. They had fought in a war, it seemed, some time in the dim past, at a place called Kerbala, and were treacherously killed – the one murdered, the other poisoned. They were great fighters who could back a crowd. Of this much he was certain; but as to what they fought for, or what the hoseys signified or stood for, he neither knew nor cared.

It was enough for him that it all culminated in a festival, a passion play with a semi-religious as well as a semi-carnival tang about it, and that it commemorated the fighting talent and subsequent martyrdom of the brothers, who, though purely Mohammedan, with Hosey itself an intrinsically Mohammedan affair, had somehow found themselves included in the vast, ever-accommodating Hindu pantheon, and occupied fairly prominent niches in the infinite Valhalla of the gods; who could grant boons, even as Shiva or Kali or Hanuman could grant boons.

But to his chums Gurudeva advanced an altogether different reason for building the hoseys. He reminded them that the honour of the village must be kept. In fact, the village had no honour, and honour must be given it. Meeting them on the bridge rendezvous, he let them know with brutal frankness that they each ought to be ashamed of himself; that, in fact, each of them ought to drown himself in a handful of water – if more water could not be had – for keeping the village in such disgraceful obscurity.

The young fellows agreed. They resolved that apart from a *gatka* band they must have a hosey; and they vowed that it must eclipse all the other hoseys ten miles around, in splendour and design. The hosey must be a replica of the Taj Mahal itself. Dinnoo had a picture of the Taj Mahal, and the hosey-maker could use that on which to pattern the bamboo framework of the two hoseys – Big Hosey and Little Hosey.

The deliberations closed, the members vacated the bridge

rails. The next Sunday, bright and early, Gurudeva himself, accompanied by two of his comrades in arms – Jairam and Dinnoo – sallied forth on a collection tour. From house to house Gurudeva and his companions went. Few dared refuse them a contribution; and the few who did refuse, pleading 'hard up', were given such a look by Gurudeva that they changed their minds there and then, and promised to give their bits as soon as they got money next pay-day.

Within a fortnight sixty dollars was collected, and Gurudeva hired the best hosey-maker to build the hoseys – Big Hosey and Little Hosey.

They were grand creations – especially the Big Hosey. It towered above the crowd on parade day. Gurudeva himself was resplendent in his *gatka* panoply. He wore red satin shorts on which were fixed miniature mirrors and hung with bells around the knees; bells that jingled with every tremor and motion of his body. His shirt was specially decorated; it carried more mirrors than his pants. He had scarlet silk bound tightly round his wrists, from each of which a length of the silk flaunted for style. Magnificently he pranced and pirouetted to the rhythmic thunder of the drums, shouting, 'Ya, Ali! Any man!'

He brandished his stick with style and gusto. He really was impressive, and everybody said so, and he was mighty proud to hear it and shouted, 'Ya Ali!' yet the louder.

But he knew that he was among his own crowd and that no one would take him seriously.

The hour was about three-thirty. The day was hot. The gallery of the big shop at the junction was thronged with spectators – men, women and children. The crowd spilled out on the road.

Then the competing hoseys – three in number – came round the bend in the road a quarter of a mile away from the junction. Borne along in procession, the hoseys gleamed in the distance. They were wonderful creations of bamboo and coloured paper and tinfoil. Each represented the tomb of Hussein. Drums thundered on both sides. With the thunder of the drums blended the voices of women raised in song. Of the valour of Hassan and Hussein, of blood and battle, treachery and murder, of gleaming swords and flying scimitars they sang.

Determined young men, armed with sticks, represented incidents in the war of the Caliph's succession. Gurudeva's cries of 'Ya, Ali!' lessened in frequency. They also lessened in tone and sting. He did not want to get into any serious *gatka* clash. He could not bear the prospect of his sustaining a broken head. He wondered what it felt like when a fellow got a whack on the head with a *gatka* stick.

There were three hoseys coming to the junction. That meant there would be three *gatka* bands. Here at the big shop, when the hoseys met, fights could hardly be avoided. The fellows who were beaten last year would want to get even this year with the fellows who had beaten them. They would throw down their sticks and issue challenges. They would even call the names of the *gatka*-men they would want to get even with. It was terrible.

Suddenly Gurudeva turned to Dinnoo. 'Look here, Dinnoo boy,' he said. 'I have a hell of a headache, me teeth

51

hurting me, too, and me wrist – me right wrist – look like it sprain. Len' me you' handkerchief.'

He took the handkerchief and bound it tightly round his head; he borrowed another and bound his jaw with it, twisting the ends of the cloth into a knot on the middle of his head. The projecting ends went up into two shoots that looked like short horns. With a third handkerchief he bound the wrist of his right hand on top of the silk bandage.

'You look,' Dinnoo told him with a laugh, 'as if you now from hospital. You look funny.'

Gurudeva shot the interlocutor a medusa glance. 'Mind what you saying!' he scowled. He jerked his chin towards the advancing procession of hoseys. 'It is lucky for them, though, that I get sick today. Odderwise I woulda show them,' he said.

7

'Ya, Ali!'

The hoseys were within a stone's throw of the junction. The *gatka*-men seemed terribly serious. They moved with agility and precision, timing their steps with the rhythm of the drums. Their faces shone with sweat. Sweat drenched their costumes till the thin cloth stuck to their bodies like wet paper. It was not altogether a mimicry representing incidents in the Kerbala battle that had been fought thirteen hundred years ago. The spirits of Hassan and Hussein were the spirits of the *gatka-wallahs*. The women were Bibis and Fatimahs.

The hosey-bearers set down their hoseys. The crowd swelled in volume. The heat grew more oppressive. The din became an uproar and a babel.

'Ya, Ali!'

Gurudeva was suddenly confronted by a *gatka*-man from one of the opposing camps. The colour left his face. The challenger thwacked his leathern shield on the left hand with his stick dramatically. 'Ya, Ali!' he challenged again.

Gurudeva strove for nonchalance and folded his arms. 'Look here,' he said, 'it is lucky for you I sick today.' He placed his hand on his jaw. 'Me teeth hurting me.'

'Ya, Ali!' roared the challenger, a tall and hefty fellow as tall and as hefty as Gurudeva himself. 'Is you I want. You play *gatka* wid you' hand, not wid you' teeth. I hear plenty 'bout you. Come out!'

'Orright,' said Gurudeva. 'I won't dotty me stick on you. You is only a little sardine. I will put one of me boys before you. Dinnoo, play this man!'

'Ya, Ali!' cried Dinnoo, thwacking his shield. 'Any man!'

The challenger turned and faced him. 'Ya, Ali!'

They walked to each other and touched hands ceremoniously.

'That is the *salaami*,' Gurudeva explained to a Chinese man who stood near him. 'It is stickman against stickman. Leh them have it out.'

'What is chalami?' asked the Chinese, puzzled.

'It mean,' Gurudeva said impatiently, 'leh we make we peace before we start fighting, because after the fight is over, one or the other of us may not be alive!'

'Leh me lun pack in me parlour den,' said the Chinese. 'Awlight, chus now police going going hold dem.'

The Chinese hurried back to his eight by ten refreshment shack over the road drain.

Stick clattered on stick eloquently. Then Dinnoo made his first blow. The challenger parried it smartly and retaliated almost simultaneously. Dinnoo took it expertly on his shield. The crowd surged around the stickmen. They cheered. Gurudeva held his stick at the ends and pressed back the crowd. 'Give them room!' he kept on saying. 'This is village against village.'

The two men duelled briskly and expertly. Each seemed

54

equally dexterous. Dinnoo shot his second blow. The challenger broke it on his stick. They duelled for about ten minutes. Neither of them could hit the other. Then they stopped. They walked to each other, smiled and shook hands.

'You good for yourself,' the challenger told Dinnoo.

'*You* good too,' answered Dinnoo.

A Donald Duck of a man began to jump and prance before Gurudeva. He was a grey-haired fellow, drunk and merry. He kept on challenging almost everybody to engage him in a *gatka* duel, but no one minded him. 'Sookhwa game today,' they said. 'He remembering he young days.'

Sookhwa was a *gatka*-man in his time, and now that his limbs were no longer lithe, he enjoyed himself on Hosey Day with rum and memories. He kept colliding with people. He could hardly carry himself.

'Ya, Ali!'

He was before Gurudeva now, and prodded him limply with his stick.

Gurudeva began to think fast. Here was an opportunity to redeem himself from the shame of returning home without drawing blood with his mounted stick; of returning home without a spot or two of blood on his gay costume.

He squared up before Sookhwa.

'Ya, Ali!' he cried, and struck the drunken fellow a whacking blow on the head. Sookhwa fell. Gurudeva brought down another blow on the fallen man's head. Blood.

'It is advantage,' someone shouted.

A dozen voices echoed the cry. A police constable came running up. In a flash Gurudeva remembered the boast of his father: Khardukhan would break policemen's heads too. Aiming a blow he struck the constable on the middle of the head. The policeman staggered. Aiming another blow on his head, Gurudeva knocked him down. Then Gurudeva could not move. Three policemen bore down upon him and held him down as in a vice. They wrested away his stick. He struggled but they quickly subdued him with their batons.

Next day, of course, Gurudeva was brought to the police court. The courthouse was packed with spectators. Most of them were Gurudeva's friends. His father and his mother, as well as his brothers with a number of his bosom chums, occupied the front bench. Ratni was there, too, sitting next to Jhulani. Gurudeva had at first objected to her coming; but on second thought had decided to let her come. Only Mira and Dhira remained at home.

Gurudeva had no lawyer. He told his father from the outset that he would plead guilty.

'I beat them and I going take me jail,' he said bravely.

He was accused of wilfully and feloniously wounding Sookhwa and of wilfully and feloniously wounding Police Constable Harker in the execution of his duty. The accusations were laid indictably, but on the consent of Gurudeva, the magistrate decided to take them summarily.

Electing to conduct his own defence, Gurudeva reminded the court that the incident had happened on Hosey Day. Stick-playing, he said, was part of the festival. People got wounded, it was true, but that was only part of the game.

The magistrate dipped his pen in the ink-well before him. 'There is no justification whatever for what you did. The man Sookhwa was drunk. You knew that fully well. Besides, he was an old man. The evidence is that you knocked him down with the first blow of your stick; then you struck him again on the head as he sprawled on the ground. As to your attack on the policeman . . .'

The magistrate turned to the prosecuting sergeant. 'Any previous conviction?'

The orderly looked into a long book and held down a page with his forefinger.

'Six for fighting, seven for disorderly behaviour, three for throwing missiles . . .'

The magistrate puckered up his eyebrows.

'And if I may remind your worship,' said the prosecuting sergeant, 'in the last case the missiles in question happened to have been addled eggs. Gurudeva went up a tree and hurled the stinking things on a tentful of wedding guests at one of these Indian weddings.'

'I remember,' said the magistrate. 'It was I who dealt with him.' He looked at Gurudeva. 'You are a rotten egg yourself. You will do six months for wounding Sookhwa, and six months for wounding Police Constable Harker. In addition, I deem you a rogue and a vagabond.'

Gurudeva glared. 'Orright,' he said, 'wait until I come back.'

'Constable, take him away.'

Jhulani and Ratni burst into sobs, but a constable at the door quickly ordered them outside. All of Gurudeva's friends walked out in file. On the way to the prison motor-van Gurudeva saw his father. The old man's eyes were red and misty with tears, but he looked bravely and proudly at Gurudeva and said:

'Orright, Guru, break you' jail as a man, boy, an' show dem.'

Gurudeva waved his hand and gave out a quiet smile. 'Is orright, Bap, I is a man.'

8

The Return of Gurudeva

When Gurudeva returned from jail it was as though he had returned from the war. It was as though he had returned from the war bedecked with medals for bravery of one sort or another. He was buoyant. He made himself look buoyant. Except that he was slightly paler and a bit thinner, twelve months of prison life seemed to have left him looking as good as his old self. His whole attitude said: 'Look, jail means nothing to me; I am as gay and dashing as ever.'

He alighted on the station platform with an agility that did him credit. He was in grey flannel trousers and in a spectacular 'hot shirt'. It was plain he had these sent him specially for his home-coming. Old Jaimungal was the first to greet him; and here Gurudeva did a thing he had never done before: he stooped and reverently took the dust of his father's foot and carried it to his forehead, as any devoted, well-mannered son should. The old man, in a voice flurried with emotion, murmured: 'Live, son!' Then he embraced Gurudeva. A tear trickled down the old man's cheek.

'Don' cry, Bap,' said Gurudeva. 'I come back; and I come back like a man again.'

Both Ramnath and Makhan, Gurudeva's elder brothers,

were there, too, and Gurudeva hurried to meet them. The brothers shook hands, then, before all the people, they kissed each other.

'So how?' asked Ramnath, in a quiet, affectionate undertone.

'Who? Me? I orright,' said Gurudeva.

There was an awkward pause. Then, as though he should say something more, Gurudeva said: 'Jail ain't bad, you know. It is only the name of jail that is bad.'

'*Shabas, beta*! Bravo, son!' exclaimed Jaimungal. 'I like how you take it.' There was no doubt about it, the old man felt proud and lifted. 'Well, you went to jail, an' you show everybody how you is a man. You din go for t'iefing; you went for fighting. No shame in that, boy.'

'I know,' said Gurudeva.

They passed through the wicket gate, Gurudeva letting the ticket-collector know, in an unnecessarily loud voice, that he didn't have to deliver any ticket. He waved his discharged prisoner's pass.

'Pass on,' said the ticket-collector, a young Negro of about twenty-one. 'Hope this is the last time you passing like that.'

'What you say dey?' asked Gurudeva in sudden umbrage. 'Leh me hear you again.'

'Nothing,' said the ticket-collector. 'I ain' say anything. Go your way.'

'Oh-ho!' said Gurudeva.

They got into a taxi.

'Bap,' said Gurudeva, after he had been settled between Ramnath and the old man — Makhan sat with the driver — 'Bap, I never did know jail was so easy. I was friend of the turnkey. Jus' pickin' dry leaf in the Governor garden. Look at me hand.' He spread out both hands, palms up. 'Sof' an' red like jam!'

'True,' said Jaimungal, who, if he had on glasses, would have seen the fossil remains of some corns.

Makhan said: 'And what about the food, Guru? Is true they does give you beef? You shoun' eat it.' Makhan spat clean out of the taxi.

'Give you beef if you want it,' said Gurudeva. 'It was fowl an' fish an' mutton an' sal'fish for me.'

'Good food,' commented Ramnath. 'I thought they woulda give you beef and po'k!'

'They coun't give me what I didn't want. If you is a Hindu they don't force you to eat beef and po'k. And when you talk 'bout food – well, it is in jail you get food. In the morning a whole big cup full of cocoa or tea or coffee. Depending what you want. And bread and butter. Good butter too. The dam Chineyman kian't tell me 'bout butter now. And the bread they sell in the shop is no good. Too small.'

Ramnath and Makhan chuckled, but the old man dried a tear with a corner of his *koortah*. He wasn't crying, really. He was just glad at Guru's being so brave and uncommon.

'If it wasn't for the family you miss in jail, you won't find jail bad,' Gurudeva said, by way of breaking another awkward silence. 'That is the only thing 'bout jail. You miss you' family like hell.' Then suddenly he asked: 'But what about them boys – I mean Dinnoo and Jairam and Ramlal and the odders. Twice they come to see me. Fust time they make me cry. I suppose they goin' rough on me for that now?'

'Not them,' said Makhan.

Old Jaimungal said: 'All the same, *beta*, I think you better don' have much to do wid them boys now. I woun't like to see you go to jail again.'

Makhan said: 'Bap is right, Guru. Keep away from those boys.'

'Who? Me? I done wid them,' said Guru.

This was not true. He was not done with them, though at the moment he may have meant it. But Gurudeva himself was not certain on his next move. His ideas were as yet more or less nebulous.

The fact is, something had happened to Gurudeva in jail, and that thing had to do with religion. Jail, he had found, was no fun. The very day after his arrival at Carrera, the twenty-acre island settlement, he had found himself pounding coconut husks into fibre. The pestle-like hardwood with which he was working blistered his hands in almost no time. After half an hour he threw away the pounding-stick and blew on his hands as though to cool the burning blisters. A tall, khaki-clad man bent over him, and Gurudeva heard the tall man saying:

'Why you not working?'

Gurudeva looked up and saw it was the warder, leaning on a gun. He thereupon truthfully reminded the officer that he, Gurudeva, was not accustomed to hard work.

The officer equally truthfully informed Gurudeva that

there were many on the settlement who at the first were also not accustomed to hard work.

Veiling a bribe, Gurudeva hinted he was not a poor man. The warder replied that jail, like heaven, hell, or the law itself, was no respecter of persons.

'You must work,' he said.

To the warder's great astonishment Gurudeva began to sing.

It was not a loud singing; what he sang was slightly above a crooning. But he sang. He sang the song that he had heard his father sing on waking first thing every morning. In a low voice Gurudeva sang: '*Natha mohi abki bera ubaro*! O Lord, this time save thou me!'

Tall, corrugated Bon-Bon, doing fifteen years for manslaughter, watched Gurudeva open-mouthed. Short, rotund, chubby Ching Fu, doing three months for keeping an opium-smoking den in Charlotte Street, the Chinatown of Port of Spain, exclaimed: 'Wa long, Gulu?' Everybody was aghast.

'What's that you saying?' asked the warder.

Gurudeva said: 'I ain't saying anything; I prayin'. I prayin' for God to help me in me trouble.'

'Oh, all right,' said the warder. 'But don't sing now. You can't sing and work at the same time. Not in jail – you understand?'

And this was how Gurudeva got religion into him. Hitherto he had little, if any, of it. Once in six months or so the old man would offer a puja or worship to Hanuman, the Monkey God. But this was not much. It was not a prayer-service really. It was simply a propitiatory ceremony to win the favour of Hanuman, who is a kind of superman, who could dissipate any evil, conquer any malignant spirit, relieve one of any ugly dreams. All that the old man had to do was to call Pundit Shivlochan, the priest, provide some well-cooked *mohan-bhog* – a sweetmeat of flour, ghee, milk and sugar – and bananas and mangoes or whatever fruit there was in season; fry *soharis* and prepare *tarkaris* of pumpkin and of English potatoes, and offer these to Hanuman at the foot of a fifteen- or twenty-foot tall bamboo staff flying a red flag in honour of the god.

Once a year Jaimungal would sit to a *Satya-Narayan katha*, which was a far bigger puja, to which would be invited all the people in the village; for Satya-Narayan was the God of Truth, the creator and upholder of the universe. And after the *katha* there would be *bhajan* or singing, and a great feasting, in which the Brahmins, members of the priestly caste, would be the first to eat.

And apart from these ceremonies Gurudeva knew little else of religion of any kind, nor did he understand, or care to understand, the significance of these things. In the Canadian Mission school that he had attended there was a period in which the class-teacher took the children in Bible lessons, but Gurudeva had never been keen on that. His father kept warning him that he must never become a Christian. 'If you do, I goin' put you out me house, boy.'

So Gurudeva remained a Hindu, and was proud of his being a Hindu, though he hardly knew what Hinduism meant.

After what the warder said to him, he did not sing while at work, but every morning before the jailer came, he would sing in his cell. He knew no set prayer, but he would sing the devotionals his father sang. He would begin one plaint that had for refrain: '*Tum bin Shri Krishna Deva aur kaun mero?* Apart from Thee, O Krishna, who else is for me?'

And he would reach a stage in the singing when it would be difficult to say whether he was singing or crying. The truth is, he would be doing both. Immediately from the tail-end of one *bhajan* he would go off into another, and from this into yet another, till the jailer would come and say to him, 'Now, you stop being noisy.'

Sometimes, unaccountably enough, in the middle of a *bhajan* a wisp of doubt would rise in him, and this wisp would grow into a dense fog clouding his faith and launching him into confusions of utter doubt. Suppose there was no God? Once or twice he had heard Ching Fu say so. Then, were all his *bhajans* addressed to an airy nothing? He would stop singing and call to Ching Fu in the next cell.

'Ching Fu,' he would call. 'Ei, Ching Fu!'

And when Ching Fu would answer, Gurudeva would ask: 'Tell me, Ching Fu, is true there is no God?'

'Aw!' the Chinese would say. 'Done with that. He awlight.'

But this off-hand cynical reply would not satisfy Gurudeva, and he would turn to Bon-Bon, his cell-mate on the other side.

'Bon-Bon,' he would call; 'you hearin'?' And when Bon-Bon would answer, Gurudeva would say, 'Look, Bon-Bon, Ching Fu playing the fool. You tell me now – you think there is a God?'

'Sure there is a God,' Bon-Bon would say.

'How you know?'

'Well,' Bon-Bon would answer, 'look at me, look at Ching Fu – look at all the people in this jail. If it wasn't for a God we wouldn't be here.'

'I think so too,' Gurudeva would say; and his confidence would be restored for a day or two, and he would go about his task quiet and cheerful, so that he was soon credited by many with a deal of piety. Some of the prisoners even began to call him – albeit facetiously – 'Pundit'. And Gurudeva rather liked being called Pundit, and he strove more and more to make his mien that of a priest, missing to his regret only his dhoti and *koortah* and puggree and caste-marks on forehead and arms and throat – like Pundit Sookhlal, his own father-in-law, or like Pundit Shivlochan, the family priest.

One day, in the middle of his fibre-pounding, Gurudeva let off a painful groan. He dropped the pounding-stick and, bending down, held his belly with both hands. 'Is a pain I get,' he cried. 'Oh, God! Me belly!' This occurred towards the end of his sentence.

A little later he began to throw up; a fever came upon him. That night he rolled and howled a lot in his cell. In the morning the prison doctor ordered him to the Colonial Hospital in Port of Spain: Gurudeva had to be operated upon for appendicitis. After hospital, being too weak for Carrera, he was for the remainder of his sentence kept at the Royal Jail in Port of Spain and was taken to do light labour in Government Gardens, sweeping the paths.

And that was how he had come to have soft hands.

★

They reached the house, and all the family at home came out in a body to meet Gurudeva at the door. Jhulani, Gurudeva's mother, led the van; behind her were Mira and Dhira. Ratni kept shyly in the rear. Jhulani hung on to Gurudeva's neck and, burying her nose on his chest, began to sob convulsively. He let her for a minute or so, then gently held her off.

'Don' cry, Mai,' he said; 'don' cry. Ain't I orright? Ain't I come back?'

She blew her nose and dabbed her tears. Then Mira, seeing her opportunity, smiled a quiet welcome to Gurudeva, and asked: 'How, Guru?'

'I well, *Bhowji*,' he said. 'I quite orright. But how you, eh?'

There was no answer to this. An answer was not necessary.

Then Dhira, Gurudeva's second sister-in-law, the wife of Makhan, exchanged a smile and a word or two with him; and last of all came Ratni. She gave Gurudeva a brief, shy, affectionate, respectful glance with tearful eyes – as indeed she should – and stooped and touched his toe – as which good Hindu wife would not, in the circumstances?

Gurudeva, looking down on her stooping form, said hastily:

'Is orright, is orright.'

He ought not to have said that – not just that, in that shameful way. He ought to have touched her on the head or the shoulder and given her his benediction. He ought at least to have said 'Live!' in Hindi. The moment and the occasion demanded Hindi. But he was shy, as shy as Ratni herself. He felt acutely embarrassed and awkward and found it difficult to say the right words in the right way and in the right language. One simply did not show one's true feelings to one's wife in the presence of all of one's elder relations.

'Well,' exclaimed Gurudeva, 'at last I home!' He yawned and stretched himself.

9

Gurudeva Becomes a
Vegetarian and Teetotaller

He left them then, and made for his little room in the gallery back of the house. Ratni had everything spick-and-span. There was a clean, washed sheet of flour-sacks on the charpoy and pillows in new cases of cotton-cloth. The floor and walls were freshly done with a thin wash of greyish earth, and everything in the room seemed to be in the same place, almost as he had last seen them. There, in the corner, at the head of the charpoy, stood his sticks, all in a bunch; and there, hanging from the rusty nail on the wall, was his *gatka* regalia – his satin shorts and shirt – looking a trifle dusty and faded, it was true, but there they were, with the mirrors and bells and all. He did not seem to like the look of them, though; he pressed his under-lip and pulled the things down and kicked them viciously away under the charpoy.

'Who the hell want them things again?' he said.

He gave a short look round, then lay down on the charpoy, not bothering to take off his shoes. He lay flat on his back, hands clasped under his head, eyes staring on the black, sooty galvanized-iron roof. He seemed to be in deep thought, or perhaps he was simply luxuriating in this new freedom. The chatter of the people in the house seemed far away and left him unaffected. They were voices he had longed to hear for twelve months.

It was good to be home again; and, oh, it was sweet to be free. He would be a different Gurudeva now. Yes, no more jail for him. He had enough of it.

Sleep began to steal upon him and he yielded himself to it as the saint gives himself to his God.

A little later Ratni came into the room, and seeing him asleep, she felt a sudden stab of pity for him, and she knelt down and quietly undid the strings and took off his shoes. Then, getting up, she whispered as she might have to a sleeping child she did not want to waken: 'Now sleep.'

It was one in the afternoon and he still slept. Then Ramnath came and looked at him. Gurudeva was sweating and muttering in sleep. He flung out an arm, and waking up suddenly with the jerk, opened his eyes. He looked at Ramnath and said: 'Oh, it is you! T'ank God! I thought it was the warder. I was dreaming. I was still in jail.'

He sat up.

Ramnath said: 'Well, you ain't in jail now. Come eat; food ready. Bap and everybody waitin'.'

Normally the family seldom ate together. Eating together was an exception, not a rule. But today was no ordinary day. The occasion called for an eating-together, as on Christmas Day or any big feast, such as a *katha* or a wedding. The eating-together did not include the womenfolk, however. Jaimungal himself never allowed this. It was odiously un-Hindu. The women must eat after the men had eaten.

The repast comprised curried chicken, rice, paratha, dahl,

and *achar*. Mira attended to the dishing out of the food in the kitchen, Ratni and Dhira saw to the serving, Jhulani stood by and supervised. The menfolk squatted in a line on the floor, a sugar-bag or two folded and put under them. Jaimungal squatted in the middle. On one side of him sat Ramnath and on the other Gurudeva; Makhan sat next to Gurudeva. Before each Dhira placed a brass platter laden with the viands, and next to the brass platter a brass jug full of water.

Jaimungal cast his eyes all sides of him, as though looking for something that he ought to see but didn't. 'Wey the rum?' he asked in an undertone.

'I bringin' it,' said Jhulani, and she went into Jaimungal's room and returned with a quart-bottle and four glasses and set them before the men.

'Now eat and drink,' she said.

The Jaimungal lot never drank openly, for Jaimungal proudly regarded himself a Brahmin, a member of the priestly caste, who should not take intoxicating drinks, nor yet flesh or fish food. Nevertheless, Jaimungal drank, and ate meat, and fish too – quietly and clandestinely – at home. So did the 'boys' whom everybody called 'Maraj', an epithet that only Brahmins could wear, be they priests or be they peasants; be they literate or be they illiterate.

Jaimungal filled his glass. He looked at Gurudeva and said:

'Today, *beta*, is a great day for we. Once again we be all together. By the grace of God we be all well. Now, *beta*, leh we eat.'

He sent down his rum, wiped his moustache and broke

roti. Ramnath and Makhan did likewise, but Gurudeva sat quietly, looking away from his food.

'Eat, Guru,' urged Ramnath.

To everybody's surprise Gurudeva shook his head.

'What you mean?' asked the old man.

Gurudeva smiled amiably. 'I ain't eating, Bap,' he said. 'I ain't eating this kind of food. I done with meat and fish. I done with rum.'

Everybody looked up at Gurudeva in utter mystification. The old man, just about to carry *roti* to mouth, put down his hand. Jhulani exclaimed: 'But . . . but . . . but!'

Makhan said: 'Well, I *never* hear that!'

Ramnath spluttered: 'Well, if you ain't going to eat I ain't going to eat either. Is for you we cook these things, and if you ain't eating, who care to eat?' He turned to the old man and to Makhan and said: 'Bap, don' eat. Makhan, don' eat. Everything turn old mas'.'

Gurudeva, still smiling, shoved away the brass platter, and stood up – 'All – you makin' all this fuss for nothing,' he said. 'Look, Mai,' he added, turning to Jhulani, 'I going tell you the truth – is a pundit I going to be. No mo' meat and drink for me . . . Just bring me some plain *bharth* and dahl . . . And put me food in me own room.'

He walked out.

'Well!' exclaimed the old man.

'I *never* hear that!' put in Makhan.

'Everything turn old mas',' moaned Ramnath.

10

Gurudeva Girds a Dhoti

That evening Gurudeva did not have as quiet a time as he would have perhaps preferred. A lot of the villagers came to see him. Most of them came out of sheer curiosity; they wanted to see what changes, if any, jail had wrought in him; but some came because they felt if they did not, Gurudeva and Gurudeva's household on the whole would bear them ill will.

Jairam was there and Ramlal and Dinnoo – Gurudeva's best friends. Jairam was thirty-five, thin and small, son of Jhagroo the barber. He did not follow his father's calling, however. He said barbering of the old-fashion type did not pay. People wanted you to come to their homes and cut their hair; and, as though this was not enough for the twelve cents they paid you for a haircut, those like Baboo Seemungal, who was India-born, expected you to cut their toe-nails and shave their arm-pits; and those who were still older, and consequently still more old-fashioned than Baboo Seemungal, wanted you to give them a massage – all this on top of the haircut. So he had given up barbering, partly to work in the estate sugar-fields as weeder and cutlasser, and partly to catch crabs in the mangrove. He was married in Hindu fashion, had three small children – a boy and two daughters – and he beat his wife almost every Saturday pay-day.

Ramlal was Raghoo the grass-cutter's son, the best cascadura-catcher in the swamps or in old wells and water-catchments. He was about thirty, with a wife, but without children. He wove his own cascadura net and, if going to fish nearer the sea, paddled his own canoe. As no other fisherman within a radius of a mile owned a canoe, Ramlal was regarded as a well-to-do fellow.

Dinnoo was a bachelor, only twenty-five. He said he did not want a wife. He was the son of Birbal the thatcher, who had no other son and was peeved that Dinnoo had consistently turned down every marriage offer that had come to him within the last decade.

'But why you ain't marriedin', boy Dinnoo?' Gurudeva had asked him more than once. 'Big boy like you should be married. It don't look nice for you to be bachelor. Why you ain't marriedin', eh?'

And Dinnoo would shake his head and say:

'I goin' tell you the truth, Guru. I ain't going lie to you. Well, is a girl I have ... Old Jhagroo daughter. Remember? She married and she husband dead. *She* is me girl. Have two child for me a'ready, just at she father. Two son and one daughter. What's the use of marriedin' again, eh?'

And Guru would give a sage-like shaking of his head and say, 'You lucky, boy Dinnoo. You right. You *ain't* married and you have two sons; I married and I ain't have no son.'

So that was that as far as Dinnoo went.

On benches and boxes and chairs sat the visitors in Jaimungal's long, open veranda. Half a dozen or so of the youngsters perched on the veranda rail. Everybody had his eyes on Gurudeva, who sat on a grocery box in the middle of the crowd. Some of them looked at him as upon a wonder; or as though he had gone up to the moon and then dropped to earth without a scratch. Most of them refrained from mentioning jail, knowing they would offend Gurudeva if they did so. But Jairam the barber's son said:

'Well, you lucky for one thing, Guru.'

Guru, looking up, asked: 'And what is that now?'

'I mean to say they ain't give you a bad trim,' said Jairam. 'They ain't give you a jail *coupe*. It is a *la chapelle* I see you have.'

Gurudeva's serenity suddenly collapsed. He glared at Jairam. 'If you don't know what to talk about, why you don' keep you' dam mouth shut?' he snapped.

Jaimungal said: 'Guru don't want to hear that kind of talk any mo', Jairam. You better be careful how you talking. Guru have a different mind now. Fact is, he done give up fish and meat.'

Dinnoo, sitting on the veranda rail, nearly fell over.

Ramlal ejaculated, 'Oh, Lor!' then quickly put two fingers over his lips to signify that he had unwittingly said the wrong thing.

Conversation languished. Nobody knew what to say without giving offence to Gurudeva. It was difficult to keep out reference to jail. One by one, and sometimes in groups, the visitors took their leave. Out on the road they discussed Gurudeva freely and fearlessly. Some said jail had 'cooled' Gurudeva, some that jail had 'tamed' him, others again that jail had simply turned the fellow into a good man.

'Good man me foot!' said Goonoo, the village lout. 'I t'ink de man jus' playin' de ass. Dat is what he is playin'.'

Old Boodhoo said: 'I think this Goonoo is right for once.' In nearly half a century's residence in the island Boodhoo still spoke nothing but Hindi, and still wore nothing but dhoti and *koortah*, he being India-born. 'I have lived long and seen much,' he said. 'Jail has neither tamed Gurudeva nor cooled him nor made him a good man. At heart he is the same Gurudeva, as militant as ever; but now he will be the crusader, the defender of the *Sanatan Dharma* – the eternal religion. You will see.'

The next morning Gurudeva announced to his father that he was done with trousers. He said he would wear nothing but dhoti. (Except on the occasion of his marriage he had never worn a dhoti; and even on that occasion it was old Jhagroo, the barber, who had girded the drapery round him.)

If this surprised Jaimungal it also pleased him. He had seen which way the wind was blowing. To have a son who was a pundit – a son could bring a father no greater prestige. Still, he asked: 'Why that now, eh?'

'Because trousers is a dirty thing,' answered Gurudeva. 'You kian't make puja in trousers. Week after week you keep in it. Dirty.'

'True,' agreed the old man.

Gurudeva said: 'What I mean, Bap, is that I want you to lend me your dhoti. I ain't got none of me own jus' now. Tomorrow – '

'Is orright, *beta*,' cut in Jaimungal. 'I goin' give you some of mine. I full of them.'

Jaimungal never lacked dhotis, although he seldom wore

one. Every religious ceremony he attended – and he was invited to all – he would receive a five-yard-long cotton dhoti, with a florin or a shilling or a sixpence piece tied in it at one corner, as *dakshina*, a Brahminic present, in addition to the cotton cloth. Jhulani would make bedspreads of them, and pillowcases; or *koortahs* for Jaimungal, and underskirts for herself and for Dhira and Mira. But even after all these uses Jaimungal's trunk would still have anything from half a dozen to a dozen dhotis.

The old man went into his room and fetched a new dhoti.

'Heh,' he said, 'jus' put this on.'

Gurudeva took the dhoti and laughed and said: 'But you know, Bap, the dam joke is I don't know how to tie a dhoti. Put this jus' over your pants and leh me see how you do it.'

The old man obliged. In a minute he was girdling the long drapery round him, right over his trousers, saying, with every movement and twist of the cloth, 'You do this, then this, then this . . . It is easy.'

He undid the dhoti and, handing it to Gurudeva once more, urged: 'Heh, you try it now.'

'You mean over me pants.'

'Yes, *beta*.'

So Gurudeva stood there and went through the motions, but when he was finished it turned out a bad job. And Jhulani and Mira and Dhira stood looking on from the doorway, very amused.

'Bad! Bad!' commented the old man. 'Will fall down any time. Try again, *beta*. Don' be shame. Is over your trousers you putting it on. Nothing can happen.'

'No; you do it again, Bap, and leh me see.'

Jaimungal gave another demonstration, and when that was over Gurudeva tried to gird on the dhoti a second time.

'That is better,' commented the old man. 'But tighten the tie round your waist a little mo'. Tighten it, *beta*, or it will drop ... Ah, it droppin', it droppin' ... It drop! I tell you so!'

'I ain't care,' said Gurudeva. 'I got me trousers.'

'Try again,' urged Jaimungal.

The third attempt was successful, and Gurudeva took care to tighten the tie round his waist this time; and he and everybody else were satisfied that at last he *could* gird a dhoti.

And with that Gurudeva went right away to bathe, slinging water over his head and shoulders and legs with a brass jug, out in the yard, dipping the water from a bucket, and murmuring, '*Hari Rama, Hari Rama; Rama, Rama; Hari, Hari*!' – invocations to the Deity, just as he had seen Pundit Shivlochan do a long time ago, when he had spent a night at Jaimungal's.

Of course the old man had to give Gurudeva a second dhoti, and Gurudeva wound that drapery over the wet one, expertly slipping down the drenched dhoti and the trousers under *that* before hitching up the crutch-piece of the dry drapery.

Jaimungal gave him an appraising look, then exclaimed:

'*Shabas, beta*! Well done, son!'

Gurudeva Erects a *Kuti*

G urudeva was significantly quiet for a few days. Most of the time he kept in his dhoti and seemed to be pondering some deep question. He would sit under the mango tree back of the house, lean back against the tree, draw his knees up or stretch them in front of him, and keep thinking for hours.

If Ratni and the other members of the household had stood in awe of him when he was a stickman and a bad-John or *badmash*, now they were simply flabbergasted. He refused to eat food prepared in the Jaimungal kitchen. He said he would not have his food contaminated in a kitchen to which dogs and cats and fowls and unbathed and unwashed persons had common access.

Getting hold of some mangrove wood that the old man kept for firewood, and salvaging some discarded grocery boxes and some old and twisted galvanized-iron sheets, he rigged up a shack back of the house, and ordered Ratni to put up a new *chulha* or fireplace in it. Ratni obeyed. He insisted on her taking a bath each day, before preparing his meals, and he saw, too, that she daubed the *chulha* with a wash of cow-dung and earth before she lighted the fire. The first time he came upon a chicken pecking some scattered food grain in the new kitchen, he promptly fetched one of his *gatka* sticks and pelted it at the creature with all his might. The missile missed the chicken by an inch.

Ratni was grinding massala for the currying of *bodee* that she had already cleaned and picked.

'Look,' he said to her in his old, bossy tone, 'you right here with your two eye open, and you allow a chicken to come in this kitchen?'

Ratni stopped the back-and-forth movement of her hands over the massala-stone, and looked at him in a puzzled kind of way and said: 'I din see it. The kitchen ain't have no door. You mus' put a door.'

He ignored her remark and said: 'Now go and *leepey*' – he meant daub – 'the whole *chulha* back again. *Leepey* it, or I won't eat the food you cook on it.' He paused a minute as though not knowing what else to say; then added: 'And look. I just nearly send the daylight out of that dam chicken. Don't leh me see another chicken in here. I want no fowl and nobody in this kitchen. Remember!'

Ratni seemed more puzzled than ever.

He stood back of her, tall, menacing, legs well apart.

She asked: 'What you mean? Nobody to come in the shack? You mean Mai and Baba and Big Sisters and everybody?'

'Yes, that is exactly what I mean,' said Gurudeva. 'Only them who bathe every morning can come in me kitchen. And them who don't eat meat and fish. Like me.'

'But I kian't stop them,' Ratni argued. 'I will be shame to stop them. Them is not fowl and dog. You better stop them you'self.'

He scowled and pulled his under-lip; then left her.

Most of that day he remained in deep cogitation, leaving everybody to wonder whether he was ill. Jaimungal was visited by an awful suspicion.

'I wonder,' he said. He was speaking to Jhulani, who sat on the doorstep mending a *cocoye* broom.

'Wonder what?'

'I wonder if Guru right in he head. Whole day he remaining quiet; whole day he thinking and mumbling to heself; he putting on dhoti – and he ain't want to see a chicken in he kitchen. I hear him jus' now. I hear him playin' hell with Ratni. I don't know what to say.'

Jhulani said: 'Don't talk like that. You should be glad you have a son like Guru. Is a pundit he goin' to be. He kian't have chicken in he kitchen. Don' worry, man; he orright.'

Jhulani was right. Gurudeva's cogitations bore fruit. Within a week of his home-coming he put up a *kuti*. That was where, he explained, he would perform his puja – his worship.

He erected the *kuti* in his father's ample yard, facing the road. Jairam, Ramlal and Dinnoo, his best friends, helped him to put it up. It was a grass-thatched hut some twelve feet square, half-walled on all sides, except for a doorway. The floor, like the walls, was of earth.

In the middle of the *kuti* Gurudeva raised an earthen altar, one foot high, three feet long, and two feet wide. Then with Jairam and Ramlal and Dinnoo he went to the bamboo patch from which he had obtained his bamboo for his stick-receptacle in the days when he was eager to be an able stickman and a don't-care-a-damn bad-John. There they cut some long, ripe bamboos and toted them half a mile to the *kuti*. They cut the bamboo into various lengths and made a continuous line of bench against the short walls inside the *kuti*.

'This is the *baithaka*,' Gurudeva told his father when he came to inspect the *kuti*. 'When I doing me puja or singing me *bhajan*, people could sit down and watch and listen.'

'*Shabas, beta*!' said Jaimungal, and patted Gurudeva on the back.

When all was finished he made Ratni daub the walls, in and out, with the earth-and-cowdung wash; also the floor and the altar, which later Gurudeva called the *singhasan*, which was another name for an altar or throne. He knew cow's dung, when fresh, was sacred; dry, it was only good for fuel. He couldn't say why it was sacred; it had always seemed most unaccountable and peculiar to him; but he had not paused to reason. He had seen it used in every important religious ceremony, and that was authority enough for him. And he knew that, more than being sacred, cow's dung mixed with earth prevented cracks in earthen walls and floors.

He draped the *singhasan* with red cotton, and placed upon it a brass image of God Krishna, and another of Krishna's other half, Radha, borrowing these from Pundit Sookhlal. At the foot of the *singhasan* he placed a short slab of stone that he had picked up in the river, and on the flat stone a four-inch stick of sandalwood. His delight would have been complete had he had a tiny bell and a white conch-shell; for the whole idea of the *kuti* he had had from Pundit Sookhlal, only he was determined to make his *kuti* even more impressive. The tiny bell and the conch, and pictures of the four-armed Vishnu and of Shiva the destroyer and of Hanuman the Monkey God, and maybe a print or two of Goddess Kali – he would obtain from Kalinath, the dealer in Indian goods, the first time he went to Port of Spain.

He stood back and surveyed the *singhasan* and clapped his hands. The *kuti* looked neat and pretty and he was very pleased.

'But I will make it prettier yet,' he said to Jairam, who, with Ramlal and Dinnoo, was taking it easy on the bamboo bench. 'You will see.'

Then he called Ratni, and when she came he told her to bring him some slabs of Oxford blue, which she used for her washing. He mixed the blue in some coconut oil in a calabash, stirring the mixture with his long finger.

Jairam, assailed by curiosity, asked: 'What you goin' do with that, Guru?'

'You will see,' Gurudeva said mysteriously.

He stood up, calabash in hand, and went up to the *singhasan* and dropped on his knees, ready to write on the wall, above the *singhasan*. Then he hesitated, laughed and said:

'Joke is, I don't know how to write *Ram-nam* in Hindi. Is *Ram-nam* I was going to write. I want to write *Ram-nam* right round the walls. Well, I think I will call Bap.'

Jaimungal himself could hardly cope with the simplest book or booklet in Hindi. When a boy he had gone through the first primer and had tackled the second about half-way. Then he had given up. He said that his head was 'too hard' and that he preferred to earn his livelihood with a cutlass and a hoe in cane- or rice-field, if it came to that, rather than to have to read and write Hindi. He said what was in his karma was bound to come his way, anyway. He was cheeky; and when the teacher, Ramdhan by name, tweaked his ear one evening in the course of a reading lesson, Jaimungal spun upon his bottom and thus most disrespectfully turned his back to the teacher.

'I ain't readin',' he said. 'I ain't *want* to learn to read.'

'Give the boy another tweak in the ear,' Jaimungal's father had said to Ramdhan; but that man had simply shaken his head to say no, he couldn't do it – not if the boy was really angered against him.

That night a scorpion stung Ramdhan, and he said he was sure that what had happened was a punishment from on high for his tweaking the ear of a Brahmin boy. In the morning Ramdhan took hold of his own right ear between thumb and forefinger and gave it a sharp twist. 'I vow,' he told himself, 'to have nothing to say to that boy, he a Brahmin, and I a *chamar*.' A *chamar*, a sweeper and worker in leather.

Nevertheless, ultimately Jaimungal acquired a reputation as a reader and writer of Hindi. And, in fact, he did read. He read the *Hanuman Ashtak*, a eulogy on the Monkey God, printed in large, bold letters in a five-inch by three-inch twelve-page booklet. He read this whenever he was visited by ugly dreams, or whenever he had a difficult problem to solve, or a stubborn enemy or a stubborn spirit to overcome. In his more religious mood he would stumble and stammer over a page or two of the *Ramayana*, or bravely tackle the *Prem Sagar* or the *Arjuna Gita*. All the simplest of simple books in Hindi. Other than these he read nothing. It was beyond him to read anything else. And if he read badly, he wrote worse. Though visually he knew all the letters in the Hindi alphabet, when it came to writing them their individual shapes and twists eluded him. He mistook a *pa* for a *pha*, a *bha* for a *jha*, a *ya* for a *tha*. They were so nearly alike. But this puzzlement the old man would hardly admit even to himself, leave alone his admitting it to others. Surely, if one could read and speak a language one could just as well write in it.

'Bap!' called Gurudeva.

The old man did not hear. He was cleaning a clump of sugar-cane back of the house, and the rustle of the crisp, dry trash drowned Gurudeva's voice.

He called again, louder this time. The old fellow came, puffing and sweating.

Gurudeva said: 'Look, Bap, the *kuti* finish. Only some pictures I want on the walls. And a *sanch*' – a conch-shell – 'and a *ghanti*.' A tiny bell.

The old man put his palms together and bowed to the images of Krishna and Radha on the altar.

'Look, Bap,' added Gurudeva, 'is *Ram-nam* I want you to mark on the walls . . .'

'Yes, *beta*.'

It took Jaimungal the better part of half a day to finish inscribing *Ram-nam* in some six places, and when he was finished only he or a very good reader could decipher what he had inscribed.

Gurudeva contented himself by making an outline drawing of the Monkey God: Hanuman flying across the ocean, bearing aloft on one mighty hand a whole peak of the Himalaya.

'Good, *beta*,' exclaimed Jaimungal. 'That is a good Hanuman.'

'Yes, Bap,' said Gurudeva.

Gurudeva Becomes a Pundit

Say, *ka* – say, *ka-kabirkane-kah.*'

Pundit Shivlochan deliberately opened his mouth high and wide to utter the last syllable. He was teaching Gurudeva to read Hindi and he wanted him to understand that *kah* had the long sound.

They were in the *kuti*. It was dusk and the little earthen lamp on the *singhasan* had already been lit; and Gurudeva was being taken in his reading lesson in the light of an unshaded oil-lamp. The pundit sat on a charpoy, his feet on the earthen floor, his elbows on his knees, his chin on his hands. He was looking down on the booklet that lay open before Gurudeva, who sat cross-legged, like a true *chela* or disciple, at the teacher's feet. He was in dhoti but nothing else. It was the beginning of the second week since he had embarked on his learning to read and write Hindi. Instead of his going to Pundit Shivlochan's he had induced the pundit to come to him.

The pundit was a tall, thin, mild-looking person of about sixty or sixty-five. He had small rheumy eyes below a bush of grey eyebrows. His moustache was all grey too; and he had a hawk's nose, pitted with what might have been small-pox some time in his early life.

'Say, *ka-kabirkane-kah.*'

Gurudeva tried to say the words but the sounds he uttered amounted to something totally different to the sounds uttered by Pundit Shivlochan.

The pundit frowned.

'Open your mouth like this,' he said, giving Gurudeva a demonstration. 'Say, *ka-kabirkane-kah.*'

Gurudeva tried again but nearly bit his tongue.

The pundit turned the Hindi primer face down. He, rather than Gurudeva, seemed discouraged. Gurudeva was not proving as apt a pupil as he would have wished. True, Gurudeva had arranged to pay him fifty dollars at the end of the course, which, it was stipulated, would last about three months; but it seemed to him now that at the rate at which Gurudeva was progressing he would have to be teaching him a whole year to earn that fifty dollars, if he would earn it even then.

Pundit Shivlochan lived in Penal, some thirty miles away from Gurudeva's village. He was beginning to regret that Gurudeva had somehow succeeded in making him leave home. Now he shook a lank forefinger and said to the pupil:

'Unless you do better I do not think I, or anybody else, can do much for you. I am not a rich man; far from it. I cannot prolong my stay here indefinitely. I have my wife and four children to see about. Lakhna is wayward, and Chandariah is too big a girl to be left only to the care and protection of her mother. Raise the wick of that lamp.'

He took up the primer once more and placed it back on the floor, face up.

'Now try again,' he said. 'I will make it simpler for you. Look at me: keep your mouth nearly shut to say *ka*; open it wide to say *kah*.'

'*Achcha, Nana.* Yes, grandfather,' said Gurudeva. '*Ka-kah*.'

'Now you have it,' commented Pundit Shivlochan. 'Now go on to *kih-kee, kuh-koo, kay-kai, ko-kow, kang-kanh*.'

Gurudeva managed it.

Pundit Shivlochan slapped his thigh with one hand and tugged his moustache with the other.

'Now that is fine,' he said. 'Now you will learn fast enough.'

It surprised a lot of people that in just two months Gurudeva was reading all the books that Jaimungal kept on his little shelf. One month more and he was reciting the *Ramayana* itself; and not only the *Ramayana*, but the *Bhagavad-Gita* too – in Sanskrit.

You might say he made the villagers bawl.

Further into the subtleties of Hinduism he did not penetrate. He dared not. He was keen – and oh, how keen! – only on his being acknowledged a pundit, not necessarily a priest, though every Hindu priest in Trinidad is also called Pundit. He had neither the patience nor the inclination to learn by rote all the multifarious details that centred on even a simple puja, leave alone the details of rituals on, say, a marriage ceremony.

After all, a priest was only a kind of tradesman, so to speak. He did a job and was paid for it, in cash or in kind, or in both. So reasoned Gurudeva, for so he had heard his own father say. His father had said, moreover, that in some parts of India itself priests were looked down on as mere ritualists – a low class of Brahmins . . .

Now Gurudeva would do a puja every morning, and then sit or recline or sleep on his charpoy in the *kuti* till noon. (Pundit Shivlochan had packed and gone.) Then he would wake up and go and eat alone in his kitchen priest-fashion, that is to say, he would eat squatting on the mud floor, clad only in his dhoti, naked from the waist up. Then he would come out once more to the *kuti* and take to his charpoy and talk or argue about the *Sanatan Dharma* – the orthodox religion. Mostly it would be Dinnoo or Ramlal or Jairam that he would talk or argue with when they were freed from their work in sugar- or paddy-field. He said a lot of things were going wrong with the *Sanatan Dharma*. And if anyone said or did a thing against the *Sanatan Dharma*, Gurudeva felt he was the man to bring the offender to book. He seemed to be ever on the look-out for such offenders.

Just now he had his eye on Ramdas. The week before Gurudeva had put up a *jhandi* – a flag – to the Monkey God. He had invited almost the whole village to the ceremony, but, it being paddy-reaping time and a sun-blazing day after days of intermittent rain, only about a dozen people had turned up. The puja was therefore not as much a success as he had hoped it would be, and this had embittered him against many.

Ramdas was one of those who had not come to the puja.

Gurudeva was sure the fellow entertained anti-Sanatanist sympathies. So he had his eye on Ramdas, who lived within sight and hailing distance of the *kuti*. He knew Ramdas had a cow. He knew —

13

Gurudeva, Ramdas, and the Cow

Ramdas was a short, thin person of about forty-five, with a prominent Adam's apple and a sharp, pointed nose. Mostly you saw him in trousers and shirt, with the shirt tail almost always out. Everybody called him 'Maraj', and in a quiet, confident sort of way he was rather proud of this. He knew it was not so much a name as an honorific epithet. He knew he was called Maraj because he was a Brahmin, a member of the priestly caste, the highest place in the Hindu social set-up.

He could neither read nor write, though he sometimes recalled, with some show of pride, that at one time he used to know all the letters in the English alphabet – all.

Knowing he was a Brahmin, he avoided as best he could doing those things that Brahmins should not do. He did not eat beef, did not even touch it; he observed the same taboo on pork or on any other product of the pig. He was careful not to touch the wives of his younger brothers, nor yet to joke with them. This, he knew, was also most improper.

And he carried out those duties that Brahmins *should* carry out. He looked upon cows as *gow-matas* – as mother-cows; and at times, in his most Brahminic moments, quite meant it. On *Divali* night – the festival of lights – he lit, like any good Hindu, at least a dozen little earthen lamps to Lakshmi, the goddess of luck and prosperity; and on the approach of the holy festival of *Shiva-Ratri* he walked barefooted, brass jug in hand, to the nearest temple and there performed an ablution on the idol of Shiva. If he could spare himself from cane- or paddy-field, he went to *Rama-Leela*, the annual pageant of Rama, on the last day of the ten-day festival, and offered a pound or so of *meethai*, sweets, to God Rama or to the boy who performed as God Rama. And once every six months or so he put up a red flag to Hanuman, the Monkey God, and sometimes a white flag, too, to Suraj-Narayan, the Sun God.

On these occasions Ramdas lived completely as a high-caste Hindu: no rum, no fish or flesh food of any kind, no cuss-word. For the duration of the puja he would perforce gird a dhoti round him and allow the priest to smear his forehead with a pinch of sacred ash. He would feel more holy then than comfortable, and as soon as the puja was over, or the priest gone, he would get back into his trousers (though not necessarily into his shirt) and return to his normal life. It would be up to him then to drink his rum – after wiping off the sacred ash – or administer a clout or two to one or more of his smaller children for their not behaving well enough during the puja, or give Mrs Ramdas a short but emphatic bawling down for her not having some of the puja things ready at hand.

All in all, he was not a bad man. He worked hard in cane or paddy-land, reared his family – a wife and ten sons –

looked after his donkey and his cow, and on the whole minded his own business.

But of late he was not a happy man. It was the cow that made him unhappy. He was more than unhappy. He felt bitter, cut-up and frustrated. Today he was in one of his sour moods. At the moment he was sitting on a short log on which he had just finished chopping chop-chop, or cane-tops, for the donkey. He sat on the log, his cutlass at his side, and looked at the cow with extreme distaste. The cow was tethered to a stump in his backyard, about ten feet away from the donkey.

It was a pretty red-and-white cow. Two years ago Ramdas had bought it from Agnoo, who lived three miles away in Bejucal. Because the cow was red-and-white he called it Chitkabari. Everybody called it Chitkabari. It was sleek and big all over, and Agnoo said it was like that because it wanted just three months to deliver calf.

A tear trickled down Agnoo's cheek. He was a short man with a bony squareness of shoulders, an amiable fellow of about sixty in a scanty dhoti and merino, his head almost bare of hair.

'I tell you, O Ramdas,' he said, 'I would never part with this cow but that I stand in urgent need of money for a pressing cause. Thou art lucky!'

'Art thou sure about this, O Agnoo? That this cow will put down in just about three months?' asked Ramdas, for he was a careful man.

'God knows,' said Agnoo, truthfully. 'Take it home and thou wilt see.'

'Orright,' said Ramdas, in English this time. 'I will buy she.'

He did. He paid sixty dollars for the cow and regarded the deal a bargain. He and his eldest son, Dipraj, led the cow home. Ramdas drove a stout stump of hardwood back of his house, and tethered the cow thereto. He fed it well. He fed it on chop-chop, he fed it on para-grass, on giant grass, on guinea-grass, corn-grass — and on quite a variety of other grasses, besides.

The cow, already fat, grew fatter. It shone. Ramdas, for some reason known only to himself, kept the animal tethered to the same stump, on the same spot, month after month, only throwing it fresh beddings of dried grass every evening. In a month the bedding heap rose high and with it the cow. Two months went by, three, four, five . . . six . . .

'Eh, eh!' exclaimed Ramdas. 'Wha' wrong wid this cow? Man say she will put down in t'ree months. Cow here six months now — and no calf. Eh, eh!'

He would look at the cow often, watching to see whether its belly was growing, or had grown, bigger. He would stoop and look at its udder, knowing that a cow developed that organ near calving time. He saw no change. He could hardly believe his eye. The cow remained as sleek and round and sweet as ever. He began to suspect that Agnoo had fooled him; and as many people as would come to his house he would ask to look at the cow.

'Look at this cow,' he would say in an off-hand sort of way. 'T'ink she full?'

Some said yes, some said no, some said they just couldn't say. Ramdas would look at the cow open-mouthed and pass one finger over his lower lip in a thoughtful, sawing fashion. Then he would curse Agnoo, and when he was done with Agnoo, would tremble to curse the cow itself; but would desist. *Gow-mata*. And perhaps the cow *was* in calf. He didn't know.

'Is a hell of a thing,' Ramdas would say, instead.

Then he called Jagoo. Jagoo being an *ahir* – an India-born cowherd – was supposed to know everything that one could possibly know about cows. He was a kind of local vet for cattle.

This Jagoo gave the cow a thorough look-over, felt it all over too. Then he looked at Ramdas and shook his head dolefully and said: 'Well, Maharaj, I do not want to hurt your feelings, but the truth is the truth. This cow is no more in calf than my own bull in its pen.'

'No?'

'No.'

'But Agnoo who sold it to me, Agnoo said she would put down in three months.'

'Agnoo is a liar,' said Jagoo. 'I know the man. What you have to do now, Maharaj, is to take the cow to a bull-pasture; and when you have brought it back – say after a month – do *not* feed it high. High feeding will make her lose calf – will make her fat.'

Ramdas obeyed. He took the cow to the leanest pastures he knew in his area; and when he brought the cow back home he was pleased to see that the animal, like the pasture it had come from, looked a good deal leaner. He tethered it to the same old stump and took good care that the cow had as little to chew as possible. He warned his wife and the first three of his ten boy-children that they 'must not ever forget and feed it high'.

'Jus' give she a cane-top or two – and some plain water,' he said. 'That is all.'

The grace of the Almighty was upon that cow. For three months the sun blazed upon it; then the rains descended, and the wind blew; mosquitoes kept up their infernal chant upon her; flies lived, buzzed, and had their fill of her. But that cow, tethered to its stump, stood its ground. It neither mooed nor collapsed. But it had shrunk. Its ribs stood out in bands. Its red-and-white hair no longer shone, but stood in scrubby, lustreless patches on its tawny hide.

'Bhagavan be praised!' said Ramdas in Hindi; 'now this cow cannot but be in calf. I took good care to see that it was not overfed. Yes, this time she *is* in calf.'

But the cow was not in calf. It took Ramdas another nine months to be convinced of this; and when he was, he (not the cow) nearly collapsed. He called in Jagoo again, and Jagoo obliged; but, as before, shook his head to say that the cow was not *garbhin* – was not in calf, never was and never would be.

'It is a barren cow that you have got here now, O Ramdas,' said Jagoo.

'You bitch! You good-for-nothing!' spluttered Ramdas from the chop-chop log. 'Now what the hell I going do with you?'

The expletives were directed to the cow, of course (which stood looking at Ramdas with great streaks of *yampi* running down its eyes). He had stopped calling it Chitkabari; it was too much of a pet name, and he could no longer find it easy

97

to pet that cow. He referred to it by all sorts of crazy names and cuss-words, the most common of which was 'bitch'. He knew bitch was a bad word for a cow, and that calling a cow a bitch was as sinful and shameful as calling one's own mother a bitch: a cow was *gow-mata*. Still, he could not help it. His chagrin got the better of him.

'Now,' he vituperated again, 'what the devil I going do wid she? Can't keep feeding she all the time for nothing. Can't sell she; nobody would want a cow that don't give young.'

Mrs Ramdas came and grudgingly threw the cow a couple of cane-tops. She turned to Ramdas. She had heard what he had said.

'Some people would sell she to a butcher and be done wid she,' she said.

Ramdas gave her a quick glance. The thought had crossed his mind too, but he had not dared express it.

'Careful!' he said. 'Don' use them words. Is a sin. *Gow-hatia*. Cow-murder. Thousand and thousand of years in hell for that. Careful!'

Mrs Ramdas, a biggish, brownish woman of about forty, with long, oily black hair and a gold ring on the left side of her nose, exclaimed, 'Chut!'

She looked at the cow again – this time with a pitiful eye. 'Look to me that starving she like that is worse than *hatia*,' she said. 'Sell she and be done, is what I say. Just common sense, man.'

He said: 'Trouble in that. People will know. If nobody know, Gurudeva *bound* to know. And when *he* know, everybody know.' He looked toward Gurudeva's *kuti*, and added: 'He have a spite for me, too; think I ain't go to he *jhandi* for sake of malice.'

Mrs Ramdas cut in with: 'Orright, suppose he know — what then?'

'Well, it will be panchayat 'gainst we,' Ramdas said. 'Put we *ku-jat* — make everybody outcaste; 'cept we feed him and all the other Brahmins and priests. Shame in that.'

Ramdas knew what he was talking about. He knew he ought not to sell a cow to a butcher. He was a Brahmin; in virtue of which fact he was made to sit at every feast and ceremony exclusively with Brahmins; and after feasting, received his Brahminic presents of silver and cotton cloth. People respected him; and this respect that he enjoyed flowed mainly from the fact of his being a Brahmin. As such it was his duty to protect cows. To sell a cow to a butcher, even unknowingly, was a monstrous sin — as monstrous a sin as Brahmin-murder itself, than which no other murder was more hell-begetting.

He shuddered.

He knew, of course, that most Hindus in Trinidad no longer paid much heed to this aspect of the matter. Times had changed. If you lived in St James or San Fernando or Arima, or in any of the other hotchpotch and polyglot towns of the island, you could be a Hindu and yet sell your cow to a butcher without anybody asking you a word about it. Or if, by chance, a meddlesome Hindu did question you, you could frankly tell the man to go to hell. After that the only action he could take against you would be, perhaps, to bring you up before a magistrate on a charge of your using insulting language to him. Even so, the magistrate, hearing the circumstances of the case, would most probably dismiss the charge. He might even advise the plaintiff to mind his own business in the future; and tell him, moreover, that he – the magistrate – might have himself used the same three words to one who could be so beside himself as to question him why he had sold his own cow – supposing he had one.

But Cacande was not like St James or Arima or San Fernando. Cacande was not polyglot. Cacande a little India, almost wholly Hindu-populated, and cows there are as sacred today as they are in India itself. In Cacande, as in Debe and Penal, in matters such as *gow-hatia*, if you offended one you offended all. Of course you were made to feast a company of Brahmins and priests, but that didn't put matters entirely right for you. The *panch* or community never forgot you as one who sold cows to butchers. Everybody laughed and talked with you as before, but behind people's amiability lurked a grudge and distrust. Ramdas knew well enough that in his own case – supposing he was caught – many would grudge him his epithet of Maraj – feast or no feast. And it was by no means easy to dispose of a cow such as his without somebody in the village getting wind of the transaction.

Ramdas shook his head.

'In this place,' he told Mrs Ramdas, 'you could only sell your cow to a butcher and still be friendly wid everybody, if you you'self is *not* a Hindu. Which can't be. Not in Cacande. Or you mus' be friendly wid the butcher, very friendly – and yet not so friendly that everybody should know. That would spoil everything.'

★

The butcher's motor-lorry passed and re-passed Ramdas's house once or twice every week. Ramdas knew the lorry well enough. It was a green-painted thing, with tall, stout pickets on all sides. The lorry would go empty towards Brasso Caparo; it would return, late in the afternoon, with one or two bulls tied closely to one or two of the pickets. He knew the bulls were intended for slaughter. Once or twice he had seen cows in the lorry. That sight had made him wince.

Yet, of late, Ramdas would find himself deliberately looking at the lorry as it passed. Then he would turn away. 'No,' he would tell himself. 'No; it will be a sin. *Gow-hatia.*'

The bearded Indian driving the lorry would look at Ramdas, then he would look at Ramdas's cow. He had, in fact, eyed that cow often, ever since the days it had been well-fed and sleek; but he knew Ramdas was a Maraj and would never sell *him* the cow – the more so if the cow was in calf. But in nearly two years he had seen no calf, and the cow had dwindled from day to day. Clearly, something had gone awry with that cow. Perhaps . . .

One day the lorry stopped before Ramdas's house. It was on the return trip from Brasso Caparo and it was empty. Ramdas was chopping firewood in the yard, in front the house. The bearded man leaned out of the cab and looked at Ramdas. Ramdas gave him one glance and went on chopping his wood.

'Say, Maraj,' called the butcher, in a low voice, 'you sellin' that cow?'

Ramdas looked up, wiped some sweat off his forehead, and said:

'Sellin' it, yes; but not to a butcher. I can't sell to a butcher. Me is a Maraj.'

The butcher grimaced in a friendly way. 'Who else you think will buy a barren cow?'

'Go, go your way,' said Ramdas, frightened. 'Don' let people see you talking to me. Is trouble you going put me in.'

The butcher said: 'I will give you a good price . . . I will give you – well, say fifty dollars.'

'No, no; I not sellin',' said Ramdas, sweating hard. 'Go, go your way. I don't want anybody to make me *ku-jat*.'

'You can trust me. I won't talk,' insisted the butcher . . . 'All right . . . Sixty dollars. Now, that's a good figure. The cow ain't got much on it.'

Mrs Ramdas came out quickly and whispered to Ramdas: 'It is a good price. It is the same price you buy the cow for. Don' be foolish. Tell the man orright.'

Fresh sweat broke on Ramdas's face. He looked up and down the road. Nobody was in sight, but there was Gurudeva's *kuti*.

'Orright,' he said, 'but go now. See me another time. Go, go now.'

The butcher-man smiled and drove off.

Ramdas sat down on the pile of wood and gave himself to a host of extremely disturbing misgivings. He looked accusingly at his wife, who was now steadily chipping pumpkin in a calabash, and said:

'Is you . . . is you make me do it.' He wrung his hands. 'Now, what we going do?' he asked. 'I sure the butcher-man will come back. I hope he will have sense enough to come by the back street. I hope he will have sense enough not to come in daylight . . . Is you . . . is you . . .'

Mrs Ramdas stopped chipping the pumpkin and dropped the knife in the calabash. She looked at her husband with a hurt look in her eyes and said: 'Don' talk like that, man. Just take the fork and dig a big hole in the yard. Make the place look like a cow bury there. If anybody ask – the cow dead, that's all.'

The eldest son said: 'Yes, Bap, leh we do it.'

Father and son worked late with fork and shovel that night. They dug the ground as though they really had to bury a dead cow in it. They threw up a lot of earth. Then they began refilling the hole, and after that to shape up the mound. Suddenly back of them something crashed to earth with a tremendous thud.

The boy cried out: 'Oh God, Bap! The cow fall down!'

Indeed, it was Chitkabari.

They both ran to it. The creature was stretched out on its side. Its legs twitched once, it frothed at the mouth, emitted a faint moo. Then it died.

'It dead,' said Ramdas.

'It dead,' said the boy, with a sob.

Then they set to digging the hole all over again.

In the morning Gurudeva looked out of his *kuti* and his belly gave a jump: Chitkabari was not in its accustomed place; at any rate he did not see the cow. Having had the full history of the animal from Dinnoo and Ramlal, he had been on the look-out to see that cow go. He knew if it went at all it would go only to a butcher. And he knew if that happened Ramdas would be at fault.

'Ah-hah!' he exclaimed. 'I catch 'im today!'

He called for Dookhwa, the general factotum in the Jaimungal household – a young, ill-clad fellow of about seventeen, with matted hair begging for a cut, and a grimy face begging for a wash.

'Go and tell Ramdas that I call him right away,' Gurudeva told Dookhwa. 'Tell him that if he don't come right away, is trouble for him – is water more than flour for him.'

Dookhwa found Ramdas sitting on a bench, looking sad, vexed and tired.

'Pundit call you,' said Dookhwa.

'What the hell he want?' asked Ramdas. 'I ain't do him nothing.'

But he went.

Gurudeva had just finished his puja and sat on his charpoy exuding a mixed odour of incense, sandalwood paste and marigold.

Without any preamble he said to Ramdas:

'I suppose you know why I call you, eh?'

'I don't know why. I ain't do no wrong.'

'You is a Brahmin, ain't so?'

'That is so. I is a Brahmin, me poopa was a Brahmin, me gran'poopa was a Brahmin. What wrong with that?'

'You will know just now,' said Gurudeva. 'I will make water more than flour for you. You know a Brahmin must look on a cow like he looking on he own mooma?'

'I know that.'

'You had a red-and-white cow?'

'I *had* a red-and-white cow. Chitkabari.'

'It was a *bahila* – a cow that *don't* put down?'

'If you say a cow is like your own mooma, you shou'n't call it *bahila*. Is not a good word. It don't sound nice,' Ramdas said.

'Shut your mouth and answer me question.'

'I kian't shut me mouth and answer question. Nobody can do that.'

'I going fix you up,' said Gurudeva, in parenthesis. 'You playing smart. Up to yesterday I see that cow from me *kuti* here. This morning it ain't there. What you do with the cow?'

'I ain't do nothing with the cow.'

'You lie. Yesterday I see you talking with the butcher-man. I see you from me *kuti* with me own eye. Where the cow?'

'It dead,' said Ramdas.

'You lie.'

'Come and see, then,' Ramdas said.

Gurudeva jumped out of the charpoy.

'Orright,' he said, 'leh we go.'

At Ramdas's he saw, to his great disappointment, that after all Ramdas hadn't sold the cow to a butcher; he hadn't sold the cow to anybody. The cow *was* dead. It sprawled on its bedding-heap.

'But it is true!' he said, very surprised.

'She dead last night,' said Ramdas. 'The hole dig a'ready. Come now, Pundit, and give a hand to help bury she.'

'Who? Me? Not me!' said Gurudeva. 'I just make puja. Kian't touch dead cow.'

14

Gurudeva Issues a Challenge

It was a Sunday, and Dinnoo and Ramlal and Jairam were at the *kuti* since puja-time. Jairam gathered some flowers for Gurudeva off the hibiscus hedge, for he knew that gathering flowers for Gurudeva was a meritorious act: Gurudeva would offer the flowers to the gods; part of the blessings of Krishna and Radha would come his way, not to speak of the benign protection of the Monkey God and of the other deities.

Ramlal split some firewood for Ratni; for Gurudeva, though insisting on his food being prepared in his own special kitchen, would nevertheless touch nothing like an axe. Any very laborious work was not for him, he said. Ramnath and Makhan had begun to grumble at this sort of thing, but old Jaimungal did his best to prevent a row.

'All-you is not like he, *beta*,' he would say cajolingly to his younger sons. 'All-you make for work in field, but Guru is different. Is brain he got and good sense.'

Makhan would ask: 'So who going work for he and he wife? Me?' And before the old man would answer that, Ramnath would add: 'It is good time to finish plant the paddy. The water in the rice-field is fine and nice. Now is the time to do the planting. We want help, Bap. I don't see why Guru shou'n't give we a hand for a day or two.'

But the old man, afraid of his offending Gurudeva, would not ask him to help Makhan and Ramnath in the rice-field, but would go himself and help plant the seedlings.

Now Ramlal, Jairam and Dinnoo sat on the bamboo bench to watch Gurudeva do his puja. He performed an ablution on the images of Krishna and Radha, apparelled them with fresh garments – a six-inch strip of dhoti round Krishna, a doll's sari round Radha. He offered flowers to the deities and put the ceremonial marks of sandal-paste on the foreheads of the images; then he swung incense over them in an earthen incense-burner that he had bought on market-day from the Indian potter on the roadside. He rang his little bell and blew his conch-shell, and everybody stood up and clasped his palms and bowed his head to the deities. Then Gurudeva performed *arti* – moving a lighted camphor on a brass platter circularly round the images; first round Krishna and Radha, then over the pictures of Vishnu and Shiva, and last of all over his own drawing of the Monkey God. This done, he brought the *arti* to his father, who very reverently put his palms over the burning camphor for a moment, then carried them to his forehead; Jairam and Ramlal and Dinnoo did likewise. Then Gurudeva handed the *arti* to Dinnoo, and said:

'Carry it now, Dinnoo, to the others in the house.'

And when all this was over, they sat and talked – talking mostly of the *Sanatan Dharma* – the ancient religion – and of the people in the village who, they said, were going disgracefully to the gutter, outside the pale of the *Sanatan Dharma*.

Gurudeva sat on his charpoy, naked-back, the caste-mark still damp on his forehead, throat, arms and chest; looking every inch a holy man and a pundit, and such, indeed, he was already acknowledged to be.

Jairam said: 'That Kalpoo daughter, Ramdayah, she going to school with she hair cut. Just like a boy. She wearing low-neck dress that making most of she breasts show up. Morning and evening she walking to school with a boy on she side.'

Grim displeasure spread on Gurudeva's face. 'Kalpoo want he backside cut,' he said. 'Shou'n't allow he daughter to walk about with she breasts showing and she hair cut. *That* is not the *Sanatan Dharma*.'

'She ain't have no right to walk with a man she ain't married to,' put in Jaimungal. 'She father ain't have no right to let she choose she own man. I tellin' you, Guru, Kalpoo really want he tail cut.'

'We going fix him up,' said Dinnoo.

Gurudeva pondered. His eyebrows arched and his fore-head creased. The *chandan* or caste-mark, having dried, broke into microscopic flakes on his forehead. He said:

'A lot of things going wrong with we religion in this village. People doing just as they want. Something must be done about it . . . A *Bhagawat* now . . . for seven days, and lecture at the end of the *Bhagawat* every night . . . We could teach the people, tell them right from wrong.'

'Now you talking, *beta*!' said Jaimungal, ecstatically.

Dinnoo scratched a naked toe. 'A lot of things going

wrong for truth, Guru,' he said. 'Pundit Biswas, the man that come from India – '

'Yes, what about him?' It was Gurudeva, alert, eager, bending forward. 'I hear 'bout him a lil bit. What more, eh?'

'He lecturin',' replied Dinnoo. 'I hear him last night. He condemning what he call idol worship. He saying Rama was *rishi* or prophet, not God; he saying a woman who married a'ready could be married again. And he sayin' there is nobody like Brahma and Vishnu and Shiva. He saying a lot of things. He saying anybody who is educated is a Brahmin and anybody who is *not* educated is *not* a Brahmin.'

'He saying all that?' asked Gurudeva, hotly.

'He saying all that,' said Dinnoo. 'I ain't lying.'

'Well, he want he backside cut too,' said Gurudeva. 'All these things he condemning is *Sanatan Dharma* – come from the beginning – is all in black and white. Me *Gita* say . . . Orright – '

He broke off and called on Ratni to bring him pen, ink and paper. Promptly Ratni brought him the things. He put the paper on one dhoti-clad thigh and began to write.

Jaimungal watched him a minute in wonder and admiration, then asked: 'What you writing, *beta*?'

Meditatively biting the end of his pen-holder, Gurudeva looked at the old man. 'Is a challenge I writing, Bap,' he said. 'I calling a meeting and I giving a lecture. I challenging Biswas. Beating him wid his own whip. He got to prove what he saying. He got to prove how Rama is not God. He got to prove how married woman can be married again. He got to prove how a man born a Brahmin kian't be a Brahmin just because he kian't read and write. He got to prove all this . . . Don' trouble me, Bap; is think I thinking.'

He lowered his head and went on writing; then he stopped and looked at Jairam and asked:

'How to spell "challenge", eh? I just forget it. Spell "challenge" for me.'

'C-h-a-l-i-n-j. Challenge. That is how to spell the word,' said Jairam.

'Sure?' asked Gurudeva.

'Sure,' replied Jairam. 'I know how I spelling. I ain't read t'ird standard just for so. I know.'

'Orright,' said Gurudeva, and went on writing, every now and then stopping to bite the end of his pen-stick.

He laboured for about fifteen minutes; then took a long breath and put away the pen.

'I done,' he said, with triumph.

'Read it, *beta*,' said Jaimungal. 'Read it and leh we hear.'

'Orright,' said Gurudeva. 'Listen. "A challenge. Look out for preachers in sheep clothing. What is the *Sanatan Dharma*? Come and hear the truth revealed by Pundit Gurudeva Sharma. At the *kuti*, Cacande Village. On Thursday 13th instant at two-thirty p.m. A challenge to Pundit Biswas. If he know his religion let him prove to Pundit Gurudeva Sharma the wrong of idol worship. What is caste? What is everything? Come one, come all."'

'A strong challenge,' commented Jaimungal. 'I ain't send you to school for nothing, boy . . . This will teach Biswas sense. He will know who he playing with. Now what you goin' do with it, *beta*?'

'Print handbills,' said Gurudeva. 'A t'ousand handbills.

Stick them up all about. Dinnoo here can stick them up . . . 'pon walls and shops and things. Ramlal can help. One of them I postin' straight to Pundit Biswas. Bet he ain't come.'

'These people, *beta*,' said Jaimungal, 'they don't know their head from their toe. Anyway, what you do there is the right thing.

'*Shabas, beta*!'

15

Gurudeva as a Lecturer

They made painstaking preparations for the lecture. Gurudeva and his friends brought in two cart-loads of bamboo from the bamboo patch and as many loads of coconut-palm leaves. On three sides of the *kuti* they put up a huge tent, using the bamboo as poles and the long, green palm leaves as the covering. A whole day they sweated to finish the tent; then Gurudeva looked around him and said:

'But on what will the people sit down?'

Jaimungal said: 'It is a lecture you giving, *beta*. It is not a wedding. The men and them can stand up and listen; the women and them can sit down on the ground. 'Cept for a bench or two for those who will be in the *kuti* with you, don' worry you' head 'bout benches and chairs. This is not a Crishtan meeting. This is a lecture on the *Sanatan Dharma* . . . Yes, only a few benches you want, and I sure Schoolmaster will lend you them. School is in holiday. He is you' own schoolmaster, and I sure he will be proud is a lecture you giving! You just go and ask him to lend you some bench. Go, *beta*.'

Mr Sohun lived in a cottage half a mile away from the Jaimungals'. The house was fronted by a strip of flower garden, with roses and pinks and zinnias. Over the wicket gate rose an arch of flaming bougainvilia. Mr Sohun, in old khaki shorts and shirt, was mooching around this garden when Gurudeva came.

'Good evenin', Schoolmaster,' he said.

Mr Sohun jumped.

He had neither heard nor seen Gurudeva coming, and it was the first time he was seeing him in dhoti. The fact that Gurudeva was in dhoti was surprising enough to Mr Sohun, but the fact that he was naked from the waist up, the fact that he had on broad patches of casté-marks on forehead, temples, throat, chest and arms; the fact that he was bare-footed – these things alarmed Mr Sohun. He looked at the visitor from head to foot, then from foot to head. Mr Sohun gasped.

'I say good evenin', Schoolmaster,' Gurudeva said again.

'Good evenin',' answered Mr Sohun at last. 'You gave me such a fright. I had to make sure it was you. Where are your trousers?'

To many of the young villagers Mr Sohun habitually retained the classroom attitude and he spoke to Gurudeva as though he were still a boy in his school. He had crossed his fifty-year span and could be disconcertingly outspoken.

'Trousers, Schoolmaster?' said Gurudeva. 'I done with trousers. Is dhoti I putting on these days.'

Mr Sohun put away the garden fork and leisurely wiped his face and neck with a broad kerchief.

'But why?'

'Well, Schoolmaster, I – I is a pundit now.'

'I see,' said Mr Sohun, and repeated more slowly and

thoughtfully, 'I see! Wonders will never cease. I didn't know
– I meant to say, you are certainly not slow. You *are* going
the pace. Let me see . . . Married at fourteen – at *fourteen*, if
you please – to jail at twenty – and now, at twenty-two or
twenty-three, a pundit! You amaze me. Besides, I didn't
know you could read Hindi.'

'But now I can read Hindi, Schoolmaster,' Gurudeva said.
'I learn it a'ready.'

'Quick work,' said Mr Sohun. 'In school you never were
keen on Hindi. Your father felt that teaching you Hindi was
only a ruse on my part to teach you the Bible. He preferred
his sons to grow up as ignorant Hindus rather than as
intelligent Christians. A strange process of reasoning. But
there you are! . . . Anyway, come, come into the house.
Don't let me keep you sweating in the sun.'

Mr Sohun led Gurudeva into his short veranda and
pointed him to a chair. He himself reclined back on a rocker.

'Dhoti is all right,' said Mr Sohun, 'but I dare say trousers
are better.'

Gurudeva, a trifle piqued, said: 'But I is a pundit now,
Schoolmaster. I tell you so a'ready.'

'What of it?' asked Mr Sohun. 'I will not do your God
the injustice of thinking that He will not recognize you in
any other clothes but dhoti. What I say is, when in Rome
do like the Romans.'

'What you mean, Schoolmaster? Rome and Romans?'

'It means that in a country such as the West Indies,
Western culture and habits are the passport to progress. You
people want to build a little India of your own in Trinidad.
You are trying to dance top in mud. It cannot be done. The

difficulty lies in the fact that you are too much of a majority to assimilate, too much of a minority to dominate. On every hand you are pressed by Western influences. You cannot be entirely Oriental, nor entirely Occidental; you can no more be entirely Western than you can be entirely Eastern; neither a hundred per cent European nor a hundred per cent Indian. You will be distinctly West Indian . . . Anyway, what can I do for you?'

Gurudeva was relieved.

He said: 'Schoolmaster, it is a favour I come to ask you.'

'Anything in reason,' said Mr Sohun. 'Glad to oblige.'

He called for a drink of water and when Mrs Sohun brought it, he drank it and dried his mouth. A black-and-white mongrel sat on its haunches at the end of the veranda, briskly scratching its ear. Back of the house Mr Sohun's sixteen-year-old son, Ellway, was noisily tacking up a fowl-run. Mr Sohun called to him to cease his hammering a while. 'It's an old pupil I have here, boy,' he said.

'Is some benches I want you to lend me, Schoolmaster,' Gurudeva said.

'Benches? What for?'

'Is a lecture I giving. Tomorrow night, Schoolmaster.'

Again Mr Sohun was alarmed. '*You*? Giving a lecture?'

'*Me* giving it, Schoolmaster,' answered Gurudeva, with emphasis.

'What on?'

'Me religion. On the *Sanatan Dharma*,' Gurudeva said. 'I challenging Pundit Biswas. He condemning we religion, Schoolmaster.'

'Well,' said Mr Sohun, 'I don't know whether I can lend

you the school benches. I would have to get permission of
the manager . . . But benches apart . . . Look here, why not
let this man Biswas go ahead with his preaching? He can't
possibly do more harm than you and others are already
doing.'

'But he condemning idol worship,' Gurudeva said. 'He
saying Rama is not God. He – '

'Well, he is not altogether wrong. It depends on one's
point of view – on one's temperament. In Hinduism
idols are permissible, but not indispensable. They are a concession – '

'You puzzling me, Schoolmaster. That is a big word. Con
– concession. What is concession? What you mean,
Schoolmaster?'

'Well, I mean you are just allowed to use idols or images
if you can't do better. It is a low – a gross – form of worship.
You are expected to grow out of it. The trouble with you is
that because you began with idols, on the principle of bottles
for babes, you want to remain with them throughout life.
They become a vice rather than a virtue. Enlightened Hindus
do not necessarily use idols, nor do they worship many gods.
But all Hindus, however numerous the gods they worship,
whatever the forms through which they choose to do so,
nevertheless believe in *Para-Brahm*, the formless Absolute,
the One without a second. The gods are simply regarded as
so many self-statements of the one Supreme. What is at once
the glory and tragedy of Hinduism is that you are no more
bound to worship through images than you are bound to
worship through many gods.'

Gurudeva was visibly perplexed.

Much of what Mr Sohun was saying went clean over his head. It was like throwing water on a duck's back. But Mr Sohun was talking more to himself than to Gurudeva. He had read widely on Indian philosophy and religion and must needs talk it out. His bookshelves carried bound volumes of Gandhi's *Young India* articles; books by Radhakrishnan, Babu Bhagwandas, and Tagore; English translations of the *Rama-yana*, the *Mahabharat*, the *Bhagavad-Gita*, and some of the *Upanishads*.

Gurudeva shifted uneasily in his chair. 'Not bound to worship idols, Schoolmaster?' he asked. 'Not bound to worship gods? Well, I *never* hear that!'

'I believe you,' said Mr Sohun dryly. 'It just shows . . . If you knew, there wouldn't be all this quarrelling among you. You would worship Rama and Krishna, or Shiva, or *Para-Brahm*, and nobody would say a word.'

Gurudeva said: 'But Pundit Biswas condemning Rama too; and Krishna and Jesus and everybody. He saying them was *rishis* or prophets, not God. He saying God ain't have no hand and foot. He saying God is like nothing. Ain't he talking like a fool, Schoolmaster? Say the truth.'

Mr Sohun pondered.

'He isn't talking like a fool,' he said. 'He is talking like a sectarian. Some people would claim to know God as He is. Others, like myself, would prefer to meet him face to face in a Jesus; you, no doubt, would prefer to meet Him in a Rama or a Krishna. The one God appears to different minds in different ways. Radhakrishnan quotes an ancient text as saying that forms are given to the formless Absolute for the benefit of the aspirant. Another text says that some men find their gods in waters, others in the heavens, others in the objects of the world, but the wise find the true God, whose glory is manifest everywhere, in the *Atman* – Brahma, Vishnu and Shiva; God the Father, God the Son and God the Holy Ghost – the one concept means much the same to me as the other.'

'I going try to remember what you say, Schoolmaster,' Gurudeva said. 'But one thing more. You think woman who married a'ready should be married again? Me *Gita* say – '

'I know what your *Gita* says, but in Trinidad every Hindu woman whose husband is dead, or whose husband has deserted her, or she deserted him – quite common features of the family structure – takes a second, if not a third or a fourth husband. Only there is no second marriage ceremony. You keep the letter, but quite ignore the spirit of the law. It's just a farce.'

'What is a farce?' asked Gurudeva.

'Tomfoolery,' answered Mr Sohun.

'Oh,' said Gurudeva.

'And all this quarrel and debate about the goodness or wickedness of caste is another farce. Nobody ever observes caste-rules in the West Indies.'

'Pundit Biswas condemning caste too,' Gurudeva said. 'Man saying anybody who can read and write can be a Brahmin. He saying he can be a Brahmin even if he father is a *chamar*.' A low-caste sweeper or worker in leather. 'What you think of that?'

Mr Sohun chuckled.

'I suppose that must be rather hard on you,' he said. 'But

a Brahmin should be a man of knowledge and piety; yet ninety-nine in every hundred of you who pride yourselves on your being called Pundit and Maharaj are, in fact, neither the one nor the other. Caste, thank goodness, is non-existent in the West Indies. Nobody really keeps caste-rules, yet, ridiculously enough, most of you keep quarrelling over caste – as though you were still in some very remote village in India. Those of you who call yourselves Brahmins are not always priests, and seldom, if at all, pundits. The average pundit in the West Indies looks a pundit without being one. In most cases the epithet is a misnomer. It has come to mean anyone who goes about in dhoti and turban and caste-marks of sandal-paste. Not ten in the whole mass, numbering hundreds, could pass an examination in Hindi that equals the test of a second-standard boy in my school. Again, thousands, claiming to be Kshatriyas – the military caste – call themselves *Singhs*, yet I know not one who follows the calling of a soldier. They are not even policemen. In the same way *chamars* are not sweepers – they are often school teachers, and so can be said to have changed place with Brahmins; *ahirs* do not necessarily rear cattle; *barahis* are seldom, if at all, workers in wood. Not caste, but the shadow of caste remains in the West Indies. Its only use here is to inflate some people's ego.'

Mr Sohun stopped talking and called for another drink of water. 'You may have the benches,' he said, 'though I should have first obtained the manager's permission.'

Gurudeva stood up.

'Thank you, Schoolmaster,' he said; 'and I hope you

coming to the lecture. Dinnoo and Ramlal will be coming for the benches.'

Mr Sohun said: 'Don't know about coming to your lecture. However, I wish you luck. I'm sure it will be very amusing.'

'Yes, Schoolmaster,' said Gurudeva, thinking he was paid a compliment.

Gurudeva was giving his first lecture; his first, because of course he was to give many more. Ramlal and Dinnoo had done a thorough job distributing the handbills. So everybody knew of the lecture, and the whole village, it seemed, turned out, and scores came from beyond Cacande too, so that the long tent was crowded.

Gurudeva was specially garbed for the occasion: long white dhoti, pink *koortah*, caste-marks on forehead, topped with a yellow puggree. He looked a pundit and a Prince Charming in one, and he knew it. Six or seven pundits, more or less similarly garbed, but aged and decrepit compared to Gurudeva, occupied the *kuti*, from which stemmed forward the huge tent. Pundit Shivlochan was there and Pundit Ramdut had come from Debe, and Mahant Gangaram from the adjoining village of Bejucal.

For these to sit on, Gurudeva spread sugar-bags on the earthen floor of the *kuti*, and on top of the sugar-bags washed sheets of flour-sacks, for they would not sit on a bench; they said that their doing so would be to put themselves higher than the gods on the *singhasan*.

A dozen flambeaux sticking out of a dozen bamboo poles

lit the scene. From the green thatch hung festoons of bougainvilia, and between these floral decorations hung mangoes and green coconuts and bananas and oranges. It was Gurudeva's idea of a grand decoration. He warned every-body, though, that anyone snatching a fruit or a flower before the end of the lecture would be put out of the tent forthwith.

'If you don't believe me, just try it,' he said. 'So don't say I din warn you. Just keep quiet and listen, and after me lecture is over you can take what you want.'

There was a murmur of approval.

Gurudeva decided to give his lecture in Hindi. During the last week or so he had made it known that he was done with English. Without saying it in so many words he had made it known that English was beneath his consideration. Since recently he had been speaking only in Hindi – even with Jaimungal, with whom he had habitually spoken in English – and, still more strange, with Ratni. And he spoke not the mongrel, patois Hindi. No; he spoke, or tried to speak, the Hindi of the vernacular weekly paper that he had recently begun receiving in batches from Pundit Shivlochan, who got these every three months or so from India. It was a clever decision. He knew well enough that his Hindi, in spite of the *Ventekshwar Samachar*, the Indian weekly newspaper, was more or less on a par with his English; but whereas his bad English would be glaringly patent to many, his bad Hindi, particularly if he applied the *Samachar's* pronunciation and intonation, would be patent to none. Those who knew Hindi knew little of it to be able to correct him; those who didn't know – well, they didn't know.

Gurudeva coughed. He coughed twice. Then he began.

'Reverend pundits, brothers and sisters, this is a memorable day in Cacande. Cacande is blessed; for in Cacande are gathered this evening the cream of the Hindu community. I thank them for their presence.'

He coughed once more, looked round him, then took a sip of water from a brass jug.

'This meeting is called so I could tell you of our *Sanatan Dharma*; so we could protect our *Sanatan Dharma*. Protect it from whom? I say protect it from the mischievous propaganda of Pundit Biswas. I think you have all heard of Pundit Biswas – '

Dinnoo from the rear of the audience shouted: 'We know 'im. He is the enemy of the *Sanatan Dharma*.'

Gurudeva raised his hands for quiet.

'That's right,' he said. 'That is the truth. But I forget. Is Hindi I speaking tonight; no English at all. I don't know English.' He went on in Hindi:

'This man, this Pundit Biswas – he is a bad man. He is an enemy of the *Sanatan Dharma*. And all who belong to his clique are the enemies of the *Sanatan Dharma*.'

Prolonged applause.

'I repeat: this man is an enemy of the *Sanatan Dharma*. He is telling the people that Rama is not God. He is telling the people that there is no one like Brahma and Vishnu and Shiva. He is saying that a woman can marry more than once. He is saying that idol worship is sin . . . All these things that Pundit Biswas is condemning comprise the sum and substance of the *Sanatan Dharma*. And the *Sanatan Dharma* is from the beginning. It is the oldest religion. It is eternal . . .

'Pundit Biswas is a fool. I challenged him to come to this meeting to prove that what he is saying is right. He has not come. I knew he would not come. And why? Because he cannot prove what he is saying ... Dinnoo, bring me another *lotah*-ful of water.'

He drank his water, wiped his mouth with the sleeve of his *koortah*, and resumed:

'Yesterday I was talking to Schoolmaster Mr Sohun. You all know Schoolmaster Mr Sohun. Most of you at one time or another have been his pupils. I have been his pupil too; otherwise I would not have been here lecturing this evening. In only one thing I disagree with Schoolmaster. Schoolmaster says we must all become Romans. I say we should not become Romans. All the same I am proud of having been his pupil. He taught me *Angrezi*, though I no longer care to speak or write in that language. He taught me geography, he taught me grammar, he taught me hygiene and arithmetic. Dinnoo and Jairam and Ramlal were going to the same school – to Schoolmaster's school. They can prove what I am saying. Schoolmaster is a Christian but he knows plenty more about the *Sanatan Dharma* than do most of you. He certainly knows more about the *Sanatan Dharma* than does Pundit Biswas. Pundit Biswas does not know anything. You could take that from me. I am not fooling you. The man who is fooling you is Pundit Biswas. But why did he turn Christian – I mean Schoolmaster Sohun? I will tell you: Schoolmaster turned Christian for his *roti* ... And, as I was saying, Schoolmaster knows about the *Sanatan Dharma*. He is a schoolmaster. He is bound to know ...

'And what does Schoolmaster say about idol worship? He

says it is a concession. That means it is proper for the worship of poor people who cannot read and write. And what does he say about Brahma, Vishnu and Shiva? He says they are the same as the Holy Ghost. And what does he say about the *devatas*, the gods? He says they are all God, but just different spectacles.

'Pundit Biswas is saying that a woman who is married can be married again. Schoolmaster told me this is only the letter of the spirit, not the spirit of the letter. He says Pundit Biswas is trying to dance top in mud . . .

'Now I ask you people – my brothers and sisters – to stick to the *Sanatan Dharma*, and not be influenced by Pundit Biswas. I beg my brothers and sisters not to send their daughters to school with their hair cut; not let them choose their own husbands; not let them put red paint on their lips. All these things are against the *Sanatan Dharma*. If a girl must look pretty, she must make herself pretty only for her husband, not for anybody else; but if a girl is not married she should not cut her hair and paint her lips.

'Another thing. Lots of Hindu boys are going to school these days. Nothing wrong in that. They are all going to Schoolmaster's school; but what I am against is that none of them is keeping the *churki* – the long tuft of hair back of the skull. I have something more to say about girls. Lots of them are getting married. Nothing wrong in that; but they do not wear *orhanis*. They go about bareheaded. Some of them are even putting on hats. Hats! Well, all these things are against the *Sanatan Dharma* . . .'

He went on speaking for about half an hour, mostly repeating himself; then he said:

'Now I am going to ask Pundit Shivlochan to say a few words.'

Pundit Shivlochan stood up.

He faced the audience bravely enough, but said he did not know what to say. He confessed that if he told them he knew what he had to say he would be telling them a lie. But he was not a liar. The fact was, everything that he could have said Pundit Gurudeva had already said it. The night was getting on and most of them were, no doubt, sleepy. He himself was feeling sleepy. To tell the truth, he had been asleep during a part of Pundit Gurudeva's very inspiring lecture. He could only say – and, indeed, he was anxious to say it – that he was proud of his being Pundit Gurudeva's *nana*, and still more proud of his being Pundit Gurudeva's teacher. He hoped Pundit Gurudeva would continue to give such lectures as he had given them that night. A lot of Indians in Trinidad wanted waking up. He was sure Pundit Gurudeva was the man to do that. He —

A shower of stones came pattering down on the tent.

Pundit Shivlochan ducked. Gurudeva looked up and then looked all round. The people stampeded. Somebody cried: 'They peltin' stone!' And before the crier could run out another shower of the missiles fell about with heavy, staccato thuds. One stone, big as a mango, fell on Dinnoo's shoulder.

Dinnoo shouted: 'All you sons of bitches! All-you peltin' stone? Leh me catch one of you – ' And he made a dash outside the tent.

Pundit Shivlochan, crying out, '*Ari, Mai*! O my mother!' suddenly hunched down on his bag-spread. The other pundits tittupped.

Gurudeva, forgetting his vow against the English language, exclaimed: 'It is the doing of Pundit Biswas. Wait leh me catch him! Ramlal! Jairam! Dinnoo! See who peltin' them stones.'

He ran out to look for himself . . .

Something moved on the thatch of the *kuti*, just over the *singhasan*. The pundits looked up.

The 'something' was making a sink in the thatch. Ah, now it could be seen. Something black and macabre, dripping blood, punching earthward through the thatch. Gurudeva fetched a bamboo rod and poked the thing with it. The turf parted, the black object fell on to the *singhasan*, spattering blood. It was the head of a hog!

The pundits scampered, fearful of defilement. The meeting broke up in disorder.

'All this,' repeated Gurudeva, 'is the work of Pundit Biswas. I know. But I will show him. I going put the whole thing in the papers.'

The next day the *Trinidad Guardian* reported:

Amazing scenes were witnessed at a meeting of Hindus at the kuti *of Pundit Gurudeva Sharma at Cacande last night, when fist-size stones came flying through space and fell on to a tent packed with people listening to a lecture on the Sanatan Dharma (orthodox Hinduism). The incident occurred near the end of the lecture, which was being delivered by Pundit Gurudeva Sharma.*

The meeting broke up in pandemonium when a freshly severed hog's head, still dripping blood, mysteriously fell through the thatch of the kuti, *defiling a sacred altar.*

Pundit Sharma attributed the mischief to unidentified enemies of the Sanatan Dharma.

The incident, far from hampering Gurudeva or his course, endeared him to the followers of the *Sanatan Dharma.* Overnight he became a celebrity. The whole community sympathized with him. They flocked round his banner. He gave more lectures. Within a month some of those who had attended his first lecture became his *chelas* or disciples. They included Jairam, Dinnoo, and Ramlal.

16

Gurudeva Falls in Love

Gurudeva looked at the alarm clock at the foot of the *singhasan* and frowned. It wanted ten minutes to seven in the evening and Daisy Seetoolal had not yet arrived. She ought to have been at the *kuti* since half-past six. So Gurudeva frowned. He was teaching Hindi to Daisy Seetoolal; also to a group of boys and girls. But for Daisy he had arranged a separate hour. He did not charge for tuition. He said he would not demean himself to that extent.

By now few of the villagers doubted that Gurudeva was uncommonly learned in Hindi. None of them could say just why he thought so. One just felt it in one's bone. For one thing, nobody else could talk on high religious themes as bravely and as well – and one might say, as militantly – as could Gurudeva. He had delivered some half a dozen lectures within the last month or so and not once had anyone questioned even a single point in his perorations. There was certainly no greater champion of the *Sanatan Dharma*. Small wonder everybody called him Pundit now, or Pundit Gurudeva, or Pundit Gurudeva Sharma; and some even addressed him as Pundit Gurudeva Shastri. *Shastri* was a title for one who was versed in the Shastras, the Hindu institutes of religion; and Gurudeva held that the books and booklets he had read all formed part of the Shastras, and therefore he could legitimately take the title of *Shastri*.

'You right, *beta*,' said old Jaimungal. 'Them is all Shastras.'

'Yes, Bap,' said Gurudeva.

Ratni was not pleased at his setting apart a separate time for Daisy Seetoolal. She had her suspicions, but Gurudeva insisted that when he was teaching Daisy he wanted nobody else in the *kuti*. He said that the presence of others distracted him and she whom he taught.

'It is not fair to the girl,' he said.

Ratni shrugged her shoulders and pressed her under-lip but dared not make a verbal protest.

Consider Daisy. She was not at all like Ratni. Daisy was about twenty-three or twenty-five, tall and slim, the colour of ripe corn. She had large dark eyes, and she plucked her brows and painted her lips and rouged her cheeks – things that Ratni had not even dreamed of doing; things, in fact, that she would never have been allowed to do, supposing she had thought of doing them at all.

As though all this wasn't enough to make her uproariously different from the other girls in the village, Daisy wore short, tight frocks that clean showed up the shape and contours of her body; and she used brassieres that jutted out her breasts in an aggressive, forward thrust that made Gurudeva take notice of them under Daisy's thin, often diaphanous, bodice. She bobbed her hair, too, and periodically went to Port of Spain for a hair-do, so that far from covering her head with an *orhani*, as well-brought-up Hindu girls do, she went about bareheaded, proud to show off the waves and curls that her hair had taken on.

And the villagers wondered how it could be that a big, pretty girl like her wasn't married. But the next moment they would cease wondering, for they remembered she was a Christian, a member of the Presbyterian church two miles away in Chaguanas. On Sundays she went to church; then was the time she wore a hat, or what passed for a hat − a patch of lace-like cloth that in truth was neither hat nor *orhani*.

Daisy spoke and read English, for she had attended Mr Sohun's school with Gurudeva; and there was a swoosh about her that Ratni, and in fact all the other girls in the village, entirely lacked. What amazed the villagers, the more so the youngsters, was the way she walked. Daisy walked as though she trod on springs. She swayed at the middle, as a coconut tree sways in a not-too-heavy wind. Her shoes had such high heels that Gurudeva had often wondered how she walked in them at all. The fact that she not only walked in them, but walked rather prettily, was a thing that quite fascinated him.

The villagers didn't like Daisy. They all admitted that she was pretty, but by the same token they all said she was bad. 'Good looks and dotty tricks' was how some of them put it.

What made Daisy bad, they said, was the fact that she had gone to work with the Americans (when, after Pearl Harbor, the U.S.A. was putting up a defence base at Edinburgh, some four miles from Cacande). She was the youngest of three daughters of Mr James Seetoolal, retired catechist of the Presbyterian Mission. Mrs Seetoolal had died some two years before World War Second and Mr Seetoolal was disabled from paralysis for years. His two older daughters had married and settled on their own, away from Cacande, so that Daisy alone remained with him. For a year or two she had taught school; then, tiring of school-teaching, she had worked as a sales-girl in Mr Boodlal's dry-goods store at Chaguanas.

Then, with the coming of the Americans, she got some kind of job at Carlsen Field at Edinburgh; and soon enough Daisy had become shockingly modern. For the first week or so she cycled to and from work like a good girl; then almost every afternoon got an American 'boy friend' to bring her home in a jeep. Then Daisy would not come home for days on end, but would get into slacks and get in a jeep and go away to Port of Spain with the Americans. When she returned old Seetoolal would let her know he did not approve of that sort of thing. Decent girls, he would say, came home immediately after work; only bad girls went away to spend nights in town. What would people say of her goings-on with the Yankees?

'But is war, Pa!' Daisy would say. 'I have to work overtime. Everybody has to; can't say no; it's war. And, besides, they pay well. Why, I often make more from overtime than from my regular job . . . Look – ' And Daisy would promptly unclasp her large shining purse and bring out banknotes from it. Mr Seetoolal would shake his head half disapprovingly and mumble he still didn't like the look of things. But Daisy, humming 'Rum and Coca-Cola', would make for the small wooden enclosure in the backyard which was the bathroom, and after her ablution – from water in a bucket – she would eat and go to sleep, and after sleep would begin to get ready to get to the base once more.

'Coming home this evening, Daisy?' Mr Seetoolal would ask; and invariably Daisy would answer, 'Well, I don' know, Pa. Depending on whether there will be overtime.' And once more Mr Seetoolal would shake his head hopelessly on his pillow as much as to say he really didn't know what to make of her behaviour.

But after the war was over and the Americans had gone back home and the bases disposed of as so much scrap, Daisy had found herself at a loose end. She had indeed fallen on hard times. During the war she had contemptuously shunned and snubbed the local boys. She regarded them as cheap, oily-looking fellows. Now she was on the rebound from one village swain to the other, but still looking very much a 'hot girl'. She was a thorough mixer, and for this as much as for other reasons was looked at askance by her own Christian community – that numbered some ten or twelve households in the village – as well as by the non-Christian Indian community.

But Daisy didn't care.

In the course of one of his lectures Gurudeva had made it known that the boys and girls of Cacande must regard it their duty to learn Hindi. He said he had discovered to his shame that not two in a hundred knew their mother tongue. He said hitherto they might have had excuses in the fact that they had no one to teach them; but now they had no such excuse. He was at the service of every boy or girl – if he or she would come to his *kuti*.

A voice near to Gurudeva asked in an aside:

'True? You will teach me?'

It was Daisy Seetoolal. Soon enough Gurudeva had found himself stammering, 'Lecture is over for this evening. I shall lecture again tomorrow.'

Then he had turned to Daisy. 'Is true, nuh? You really want to learn Hindi? I kian't believe it.'

'It is true, though,' said Daisy. 'I mean it.'

Gurudeva took a walk with her – to her home – and found himself saying again and again, 'Come tomorrow, Daisy; come tomorrow.'

And she came.

From the outset he found her a prodigy at Hindi. He had to show her a thing but once and she never forgot it. Jaimungal had been watching them, and at the end of a week Gurudeva had found himself saying to the old man, 'Bap, well, I never see a girl like that. She have a good head. In t'ree weeks I going to make she as able as meself, for I have only to teach she once and she up and know it as good as me, sometimes even better.'

Jaimungal said: 'Careful, *beta*. Look to me like she know to read a'ready. Look to me she only pretending she ain't know. Look to me it is a man she want. Careful, *beta*; you have a wife.'

Gurudeva laughed. 'You making joke, Bap,' he said. 'You think is that I thinking? I ain't thinking that yet.'

The old man scratched his chin, and Ratni, passing by, stopped for just a second.

'Fact is,' Jaimungal said. 'She is a Chrishtan. I wonder, *beta* . . .'

'You mean 'bout she turning a Hindu?' asked Gurudeva. 'You leave that to me, Bap.'

The old man walked away with a troubled look in his eyes.

The hands of the clock now pointed to eight o'clock . . . There was the sound of approaching footsteps. Gurudeva sighed with relief: it was Daisy. She knew by now that she had to slip her shoes off before entering the *kuti*. This she did. She knew, too, that she must sit flat on the ground on the bag-spread, her legs drawn in under her skirts, facing Gurudeva. With consummate care she managed this too. She smiled, quietly, shyly, meaningfully. The smile said: 'Well, I *have* managed it, and you haven't seen a thing!'

'Where you been?' asked Gurudeva. 'God, I thought you wasn't coming. I thought – '

'It was Pa,' said Daisy. 'He kept me back.'

'He – he ain't stopping you, Daisy?' asked Gurudeva, with great concern. 'Tell me, because if it is that, I is just the man to go to him. I is just the man to tell him to he face what I feel about you. What you saying, Dais?'

'Careful,' said Daisy. 'You' wife watching.'

Ratni stood before the kitchen and gave Daisy an accusing look. In the dull light cast on her by the oil-lamp, Ratni's figure was a silhouette.

Gurudeva looked at her and scowled.

'What you doing there?' he asked. 'Go inside. Go away!'

'I watchin' all-you,' said Ratni. 'I seein' what all-you doin'. I ain't blind.'

Gurudeva made to get up, but before he could do so Ratni stamped her foot and jerked her chin towards them and disappeared into the kitchen.

'Hell wid she!' said Gurudeva. Then on Daisy's slate he wrote in Hindi: 'I love you. Do you love me?' He handed her the slate, saying, 'Now, try and read that and write down the answer – the true answer.'

Daisy read the sentence, broke into a giggle, covered her face with both hands as though shamed to suffocation.

'You, eh!' she said. 'You too bad.'

'That is not the answer,' said Gurudeva. 'I waiting for the answer – the true answer.'

'You can't have two wives in this country,' Daisy said. 'Jail for that.' She laughed out again.

He asked: 'You mean Ratni?'

She said: 'And who else?'

'Chut!' said Gurudeva. 'You shouldn't mind she. She is not me legal wife. Bamboo wedding.'

Once more she broke into a giggle, once more she covered her face with both hands, once more she exclaimed, 'You too bad!'

Gurudeva blew out the lamp.

A little later Jaimungal came out and stood on the step of the big house and, looking towards the *kuti*, called: 'But, eh-eh, *beta*! All-you in the dark. How all-you can read in the dark, eh?'

He came to the *kuti* and handed Gurudeva a box of matches. 'Light that lamp, *beta*,' he said.

'Yes, Bap,' said Gurudeva; 'it was the wind.'

'I know,' said Jaimungal, turning to regain the house.

They started the lesson afresh; then Gurudeva decided to reach Daisy home.

Daisy opened wide her eyes and said: 'But what will the people say? You walking with me – in dhoti, too, and at night time.'

He said: 'Leh them say anything. I don't care.'

It may not have been Gurudeva's deliberate intention to make a row with Ratni, not that same evening at any rate; but a row with her he did make, and it came about in a peculiarly spontaneous way.

He had returned after seeing Daisy home, and was sitting before his little table in his room; and, perhaps he had nothing to do just then, his mind somehow ran on to his father-in-law, Pundit Sookhlal; and as he thought of Pundit Sookhlal his eyebrows knitted and he heard himself saying, 'The donkey!' He spat out the expletive as he might have spat out two hot, putrid bits of potato. There was a sheet of paper on the table, and a stub of pencil, and in a rather doodling way he found himself writing –

The Donkey

He thought over this and found, to his great satisfaction, that Pundit Sookhlal was indeed much like a donkey. Pundit Sookhlal, he found, was stupid like a donkey, grey as a donkey, pot-bellied as a donkey. Then, without knowing it perhaps, he began thinking of the other members of Ratni's family, in sequence, and the next thing he wrote down on the paper before him was –

The Old She-Fox

'Ha!' he exclaimed. 'She is a fox!'

It is true he had never seen a real fox, but he had seen a picture of that animal in his *McDougall's First Reader* and he knew from the story in the book that foxes were notoriously cunning creatures, and nothing could beat him off the conviction that Phulmati was cunning and mean.

A moment ago he was hating every member of his wife's family with a burning hatred; now he wanted to be fair. He was careful not to let his prejudices interfere with his fitting the right animal to the right person. He went to work with the detachment of a scientist spotting his microbes without getting himself into a jitter. He was getting a great deal of fun out of the exercise. He went on writing and soon enough had produced the following list:

> *The Old She-Fox*
> *The Old Donkey*
> *The Scorpion*
> *The Thug*
> *The Human*
> *The Hippo*
> *The Donkey*
> *The Donkey*
> *The Donkey*

He put down the pencil and sighed his satisfaction. He knew that in two cases he could find no animal or non-human counterparts. A thug was not an animal, but he could think of nothing apter when it came to the husband of Ratni's eldest sister; and when he came to think of this woman herself – well, he simply had to let her pass as human: he could find no fault in her.

Ratni came in.

It was never her way to want to know what he was doing. There ever had been something forbidding in Gurudeva's attitude that rendered such curiosity superfluous and offensive, a sign of bad manners. So, without a word she began to slip off her outer garment preparatory to her going to sleep.

He said, without looking at her: 'Don' sleep yet. Is something I write here. Listen to it. I get a lot of fun writing it.'

She hung her skirt and bodice on a nail on the wall and sat down on the charpoy.

'What is it? I listening,' she said.

He read out the list, and she asked: 'But what is all that? Fox and donkey and scorpion? I kian't make out a thing.'

He said: 'Well, I going tell you. Listen. The old donkey. That is your father. He just like a donkey, ain't so? I ain't making no joke. I try to fit him exactly where he belong, and I find your father is exactly a donkey.'

She made no answer. She knew it would be looking for trouble if she contradicted him; but she took courage and said in a mild abandon, 'Orright, me father is a donkey; but don't tell me; tell him.'

He said: 'But listen to the rest. I telling you is a pleasure I get writing them.'

She said, lying down, 'I ain't want to hear no more. I hear enough a'ready. Let me sleep. Is tired I tired.'

He was adamant. 'No; listen to what I saying. Listen or I going do for you right now.'

She sat up.

'"The old she-fox",' he read aloud. 'That is your mother. Ain't she just like a old she-fox? I ain't 'zaggerating. Promise me land, promise me house, promise me shop: promise me this and promise me that. Never give a thing. She think she smart; but she is just a dam old fox – stingy like hell.'

Ratni said not a word; just propped her chin on her hand, looking down at her feet, brows down.

'Then your brother,' said Gurudeva. 'I put him down as a scorpion. He *is* a scorpion. Don't talk much, but you never know when he going up and sting you. Want everything for heself; don't care a fart 'bout anybody else.

'Well, I sorry I kian't place your smaller brother, so I just put him down as a thug. Kian't think of any animal that is exactly like him. He is *just* a thug. Want to fool everybody and take everything for heself. Full of sweet-mouth. Want to be boss. Boss me eye!'

He blew his nose and added: 'Then he wife. Fact is, I kian't find nothing against she. She is a good woman. Well, I let she pass as a human. But your third brother . . . Mohana . . . I put him down as a hippo. Hippo is a animal. Well, he big like a hippo, stupid like a hippo, tough like a hippo. He is a hippo, he wife is a donkey . . . Then them two sisters of yours – Durgi and Rajiah – them is donkeys, too. Your family full of donkeys . . . Let me see . . . one donkey, two donkey, three donkey, four donkey. Altogether four donkeys; then one fox, one scorpion, one thug, one human, one hippo . . .'

Ratni began to cry.

'You forget me,' she said. 'You shou'n't forget me.'

And suddenly Gurudeva found it difficult to say what he had to say — which was to tell her to go away — to tell her that he no longer wanted her. When he came to think of it, he found no fault in her — except for the one fault — the fault from which other faults flowed: she did not bear him a son; she did not bear him even a daughter; she seemed incapable of bearing a child.

'I don't know . . . You think you will ever have a son?' he asked.

'I is not God,' she said.

'In we religion a man who din have a son could have more than one wife. You know that. If a man ain't have a son he going straight to hell. You know that too.'

She nodded to say yes. 'Is Daisy you talking about, ain't so?'

'Is Daisy I talking about,' he said, 'and I glad you know it. What about she? She ain't bad. What you saying, eh?'

Ratni rebelled, but her rebellion had nothing very volatile in it. She knew she was in the wrong. She knew she ought to bear sons; she knew she could bear no children. She had tried every device: she had secretly prayed to the Monkey God; secretly, too, she had fasted every Sunday for months, and offered ablutions of pure milk to the Sun God; not a *Shiva-Ratri* had gone by but she had gone to the temple of God Shiva and begged for the boon of a son. And not only she had acted on these devices, but Gurudeva himself had done so; and Gurudeva's mother, Jhulani, and her own mother, Phulmati. None of them had kept it a secret from her. But the boon had not been granted. All the gods had turned a deaf ear.

'When you bringing she?' she asked.

He said: 'I don't know. Any day.'

'Well,' she said, 'you can bring she. Is pack I going to pack; is me mooma and me poopa I going back to.'

He said: 'I ain't telling you to go; but if you *want* to go, I ain't stopping you either. All the same, leh me tell you – if you go you ain't coming back. Understand that. Don't say I din warn you. Orright.'

For reply Ratni began to pack her cardboard suitcase – the same suitcase that she had brought from her mother's on the morning following her marriage with Gurudeva. There wasn't much to pack, and when she was finished she spread some old jute sackings on the earth floor and went to sleep thereon, leaving the bed to Gurudeva alone.

In the morning Jaimungal, Jhulani, Mira and Dhira, Ramnath and Makhan, all stood round her, begging her not to go; but she only kept weeping and blowing her nose and wiping her tears with her *orhani* and saying, 'Is orright, Mai; is orright, Bap; let Daisy stay with him. I kian't live with him and another woman. Is either me or she.'

As for Gurudeva – he merely said, rather stiffly and indifferently, to the old man: 'Don't beg she, Bap. If she want to go, let she go. If she kian't live with me and Daisy, she can go back to she mooma. A man is not a man if he ain't got a son; and she – well, what I going do with she, Bap?'

The old man understood; had understood the situation all

along; and, understanding, he knew he could not say nay.

'Well,' he said, 'it is not wrong for a man to have mor'an one wife, more so if he got no son. All the same, *beta*, people will laugh. It is – '

'Let them laugh, Bap,' said Gurudeva. 'I don't care. I not doing anything against me religion. I can prove it.'

But Ratni had gone.

Two days later Gurudeva brought in Daisy. The following week Pundit Sookhlal called up a panchayat against Gurudeva, for the latter's wrongfully putting away Ratni and, still more wrongfully, bringing in her place another wife.

17

Gurudeva Becomes a Bachelor

Gurudeva went to the panchayat armed with a copy of the *Ramayana*. He came in dhoti and *koortah*; and, in the fashion of priests (who must not touch leather with their hands lest those hands become unclean), in unlaced shoes. No socks. A peacock's feather adorned his silken yellow turban; and he wore resplendent caste-marks and no fewer than three rosaries.

The members of the panchayat were already in their place. They sat in Pundit Sookhlal's commodious *kuti*, and included Pundit Shivlochan, who had officiated at the nuptials of Gurudeva and Ratni, Sadhu Lalram, the temple-keeper; Mr Jagat Singh, the village provision shopkeeper; Jhagroo, the village barber; Gopisingh, a respected and respectful cane-farmer; Sardar Ramsaroop, foreman of labourers on the neighbouring sugar estate; Kuru Swami, the Madrasi palmist; Pundit Harikul, who was reputedly the best astrologer in the village.

Gurudeva 'ahemmed' as much as to say, 'I am here.'

He made an obeisance to the panch and an additional obeisance to Pundit Shivlochan. He hardly looked at Pundit Sookhlal and Pundit Sookhlal hardly looked at him. Pundit

Shivlochan shifted nearer to Sadhu Lalram and beckoned Gurudeva to a seat.

At a word from her father Ratni came, her *orhani* drawn well down her face. Without looking at anybody she made straight for Gurudeva and stooped and touched his feet.

Gurudeva simply looked down at her, muttering in surprise, 'Eh! Eh!' Then, catching himself, he mumbled his benediction in the one word, 'Live!'

Ratni withdrew. In that act alone she had vindicated her honour as a wife; she had shown to the panch that she knew her wifely duty; that she was a wife indeed.

Pundit Sookhlal's yard was thronged with men and women. They stood around the *kuti*, waiting to hear what would happen, for the case was known to all.

Pundit Shivlochan was chief of the panch. That place had been given him by virtue of his rank – the foremost of the priests in the island, as well as the most learned. Pundit Shivlochan now passed two fingers over his thin, grey moustache and said:

'The hour is late; nearly three o'clock by the position of the sun. I take it those who should be present are present. Let us begin.'

Pundit Sookhlal called for Ratni again; she came, followed by Phulmati, her mother, and her eldest sister, Roopani. She was deliberately simply clothed, and it was difficult to say whether she was shy or sad. She was probably both.

Except for some exclamatory remarks by Gurudeva the proceedings were conducted wholly in Hindi.

The temple-keeper said: 'Let Pundit Sookhlal speak first. It is he who has called the panchayat.'

Pundit Sookhlal stood up. He was in a dhoti and a merino. 'Most of you who are present this afternoon,' he began, 'were also present when my Ratni was married to Gurudeva, a long, long time ago.'

Some members of the panchayat nodded.

'He was a mere boy then, she a merer girl, a child. For all these years there has been no complaint whatever against my Ratni. She has been a model wife, a model daughter-in-law, a model sister-in-law in the house of Jaimungal.'

'We know that,' said the shopkeeper, with an accusatory look at Gurudeva.

'She has nobly put up with a lot,' continued Pundit Sookhlal. 'A lot of beatings and other ill-treatment, mostly at the hands of this Pundit Gurudeva – '

'A man,' said the shopkeeper, with another accusatory look at Gurudeva, 'should not beat his wife.'

'Why,' asked Gurudeva, half rising, 'why you don' keep you' dam mouth shut? Why you 'terrupting?'

Pundit Shivlochan raised both hands to heaven and said: 'No *Angrezi*, please! I do not understand *Angrezi*.'

'I tell you,' resumed Pundit Sookhlal, 'that once Gurudeva thoroughly beat up my Ratni, yes; then he made her open the palms of both hands, and when she had done that, he compelled her to spit on both hands, and she spat on both hands, and he compelled her to lick the spittle, and she licked it. I say it to his face; let him deny it if he can.'

Gurudeva gave Pundit Sookhlal a cutting look, but denied nothing.

'But now – now, O members of the panch,' exclaimed Pundit Sookhlal, 'Pundit Gurudeva has seen fit to put my

Ratni away; he has seen fit to put her away in order to take unto him – would you believe it? – another woman.'

All the members of the panchayat looked at Gurudeva, as though they could not believe all this without looking at him.

Sardar Ramsaroop exclaimed: 'Ho! Ho!'

Sadhu Lalram said: 'That *is* bad.'

Kuru Swami put in: 'I will look at the girl's hands when all this is over!'

Mr Jagat Singh, the shopkeeper, said: 'The spit-and-lick story makes me feel to throw up.'

When these interruptions subsided, Pundit Sookhlal said: 'Thus far have you heard me, O Panch. I have called the panchayat in accordance with the *dharma*. Let Pundit Gurudeva show just cause why he should put away my Ratni.'

Pundit Shivlochan turned to Ratni. 'You have heard all that your father has said about your husband Pundit Gurudeva?'

Ratni nodded.

'Is everything that your father says true?'

She nodded again.

'He beats you a lot?'

'He used to.'

'He made you spit on your open hands and then lick it up?'

She nodded once more.

'That is bad,' said the shopkeeper, in English.

Gurudeva said, in English too: 'You ain't have no right to say that. You ain't she husband.'

Pundit Shivlochan said: 'No *Angrezi*. I do not understand

146

it. I think it is time we heard Pundit Gurudeva. Is it true you have taken another woman?'

Gurudeva stood up.

'It is true,' he said. 'It is true and I want to see who can prove I have done wrong.'

The shopkeeper frowned. 'Let us hear you prove it,' he said, challengingly.

Gurudeva decided to adopt the Socratic method. He did not know, of course, what the Socratic method was, but he had many times listened to police court proceedings at Chaguanas and knew how clever lawyers tripped and trapped witnesses on the witness stand just by a series of rapid questions and the answers they got thereto. He would put Pundit Sookhlal to shame and to owning defeat by a similar method of procedure.

'I will prove it,' he reiterated in his best Hindi. 'I crave the indulgence of the panch to permit me to ask a few questions. It is not necessary for me to make a speech, long or short.'

Pundit Shivlochan nodded assent.

Gurudeva held up the *Ramayana* in one hand.

'I suppose you all know what is this book I have here?'

Pundit Shivlochan peered closely and carefully; so did everybody else.

'Why,' said Pundit Shivlochan, 'as near as I can make out, it seems to be a copy of the *Ramayana*.'

Jhagroo, the barber, who did not know a letter in any language, echoed, ' . . . a copy of the *Ramayana*.'

Mr Jagat Singh, the shopkeeper, said: 'I do not see what

all this has to do with the complaint against Pundit Gurudeva.'

'Shut up!' exclaimed Gurudeva. 'If you do not have sense enough to see what I am driving at, why do you not just keep quiet?'

The shopkeeper said: 'I have not come here to keep quiet just to please you . . .'

Gurudeva ignored this last rejoinder of the shopkeeper's. 'You have guessed right,' he said to Pundit Shivlochan. 'Is it a good book or a bad book – this *Ramayana*?'

'He is just wasting everybody's time,' grumbled the shopkeeper.

'It is a holy book,' said Pundit Shivlochan. 'Everybody knows that. It is a book in which God Rama speaks.'

Gurudeva nodded as much as to say, 'Just go on answering like that till you admit just what I want you to admit.'

'It tells of King Dasaratha, does it not?'

'That it does,' replied Pundit Shivlochan.

'Was he a good man or a bad man?'

Pundit Shivlochan, staring into vacancy, considered the question; the shopkeeper slowly scratched his knee above his khaki trousers; the barber looked to Pundit Shivlochan.

'Assuredly King Dasaratha was a good man, a lover of the *dharma*, protector of his subjects, the father of God Rama.'

'Good! Good!' said Gurudeva; then asked: 'How many wives had he?'

'Three wives, of course.'

'All under one roof?'

'Yes, of course.'

'Why did he have as many as three wives?'

The shopkeeper looked cross.

Pundit Sookhlal appealed to Pundit Shivlochan. 'Surely we cannot have such questions asked in reference to King Dasaratha,' he said.

Pundit Shivlochan said: 'He has asked a question. He deserves an answer. I shall give him the answer: King Dasaratha had three wives because he had no son. If his first queen had given him a son, he probably would not have had other queens. He had three queens in the hope that one or the other might bear him a son.'

'*Shukriya*! Thank you!' said Gurudeva. 'You admit, then, that a man, being heirless, is justified in his having more than one wife?'

'He is justified,' said Pundit Shivlochan.

'He is justified,' mumbled the barber.

'Then, O Panch, I have done no wrong,' Gurudeva said. 'My position is exactly what was King Dasaratha's position. As you all know, Ratni bears me no son. She is not a childbearing woman.'

Gurudeva was about to sit down, when the shopkeeper said:

'But, unlike you, King Dasaratha did not put away one wife every time he brought another. He kept all three. *You*, on the other hand, have put away Ratni.'

Gurudeva straightened up. 'You lie,' he shouted.

The shopkeeper stood up too. 'If you call me a liar, I will break your mouth,' he told Gurudeva. He began to roll up his shirt-sleeve.

Gurudeva went to roll his sleeve, too; then, realising it

could not be done, since what he wore was a *koortah* with tight cuffs, he instead dashed off his turban.

Pundit Sookhlal said to Pundit Shivlochan: 'You see what kind of man this fellow is,' meaning Gurudeva. 'He utterly disrespects the panch.'

'Disrespects the panch,' echoed the barber.

Pundit Shivlochan said to Gurudeva and the shopkeeper: 'If you gentlemen insist on your beating up one another, the panchayat may as well be quashed. Sit down, Pundit Gurudeva! Sit down, Mr Jagat Singh!'

They sat down, breathing hard, clenching and unclenching their fists, each singeing the other with his hot look.

'What were you saying?' Pundit Shivlochan asked Gurudeva. 'What was the row about?'

'He as good as called me a liar. He said I had driven away Ratni.'

'And you did not?'

'I did *not*. She came away of her own accord. She refused to live with another wife of mine.'

Pundit Shivlochan shook his head in a puzzled way. 'The affair takes on an altogether different complexion,' he said.

He called for Ratni. She came, her gaze on the ground.

'Is it true, O daughter, that Pundit Gurudeva did *not* drive you away?'

'He did not drive me away,' said Ratni.

'Did *you* leave him?'

'Yes, *Nana*,' said Ratni.

'Why?'

'He was bringing another woman.'

'It is your own fault, then,' said Pundit Shivlochan. 'You ought not to have left his care and protection. He was bringing, and in fact has since then brought, another wife. That was none of your business. Even if you had given him sons, that was none of your business. But you have borne him no son. You may go.'

Slowly, without a word, without raising her glance to any, Ratni turned and left the panch.

To his fellow-members of the panchayat Pundit Shivlochan said: 'A man may have more than one wife. In this case it is unfortunate, of course, but it is not wrong. This is my view.'

'My view,' said the barber.

The other members of the panch signified agreement.

Pundit Sookhlal stood up. He brought his hands together in a gesture of obeisance as well as of entreaty.

'I abide by the decision of the panch,' he said. 'The panch knows. But one thing more – '

The panch looked up. The shopkeeper cast a quick, suspicious glance at Gurudeva.

'I want to draw the attention of the panch to the fact that the woman that Pundit Gurudeva has taken as wife – she – she is a Christian.'

There was a murmur of surprise and disapproval.

'She wears hat,' added Pundit Sookhlal.

The murmur grew into a hum and commotion, as bees suddenly disturbed in a hive.

The barber passed his hand over his head as though to make sure *he* did not have a hat on.

' . . . and short, tight frocks, and high-heeled shoes,' said

Pundit Sookhlal, still bowing and holding his hands together before the panch.

Pundit Shivlochan looked at Gurudeva as though he couldn't believe it was Gurudeva he was looking at. 'Is all this true?' he asked.

Gurudeva floundered for an answer. Nervously he began fingering his rosary. If he said yes he would be condemning himself; he could not say no: the facts about Daisy were too well known.

'Do not insult the panch by your silence,' shouted the shopkeeper. 'Answer the question.'

Still Gurudeva made no comment.

'Is it true that this woman eats cow's flesh and pig's flesh?' asked Pundit Shivlochan, his eyes opening bigger and his brows bunching together.

'Not since I took her as wife,' Gurudeva said. 'She no longer eats any kind of meat.'

'But she still wears *Angrezi* clothes and high-heeled shoes?' asked the shopkeeper. 'She still cuts her hair like a boy's and paints her cheeks and lips and – '

'Well – well, yes,' said Gurudeva; 'but not for long. I shall turn her into a Hindu. She will wear *chappals* instead of shoes; she will let her hair grow long once more. She will neither paint her cheeks nor go about bareheaded. She will wear *orhani*.'

Pundit Shivlochan looked at the other members of the panch as much as to say, 'Well, what do you say to this?'

The shopkeeper arched his brows and asked: 'But how can such a thing be done? How can a Christian become a Hindu? It is against the *dharma*.'

Gurudeva, once more forgetting he was not to talk in English, blurted out: 'You talking nonsense. You just showing spite because you want Daisy for yourself. I know. I know you was she boy friend. But she give you up. She ain't want you any more. She – besides, you don't know what you talking. You just don't know that these days a Christian can turn Hindu . . . Look at Mungroo. Ain't Mungroo was a Christian too? But ain't he come back a Hindu so as to teach in the Mahasabha school? If you don't know what you talking 'bout why don't you keep you' mouth shut? These days Christian can turn Hindu.'

'It is true,' said Pundit Shivlochan. 'I have seen it done.'

'It is true,' commented the barber.

The other members of the panch nodded. The proposition would be all right, providing –

'Providing,' put in the shopkeeper, 'that the woman forthwith gives up her *Angrezi* ways.'

Sadhu Lalram asked: 'But what if she does not carry out the wishes of the panch? In this country – '

The shopkeeper said: 'If the woman refuses to comply with the wishes of the panch – if she refuses, Pundit Gurudeva must disown her at once. If he does not disown her – if he does not put her out of his house – he may regard himself as being deemed a *ku-jat*, an outcaste, by the panch.'

Pundit Shivlochan asked Gurudeva:

'You have heard. What do you say to that?'

'It is good,' said Gurudeva, wiping his brows.

★

But it wasn't good. For when Gurudeva told Daisy what had happened at the panchayat – how, after winning the first round he had lost the second that came up, rather unexpectedly, because of the cunning of Pundit Sookhlal; and how the panch had ordered him to see that she discard her hat and take on *orhani*, and walk in *chappals* instead of shoes, and to let her hair grow long, and to wear long skirts, and to give up the use of rouge and lipstick – when he had told Daisy all this, Daisy took a deep breath, jammed her hands against her waist, flashed a contemptuous look at Gurudeva and said:

'Well! They must be nuts!'

Gurudeva looked pained and puzzled. Clearly, he had not expected Daisy would be so utterly uncompromising.

'Don't talk so, Dais,' he said cajolingly. 'If you don't do what they say, is trouble you going get me in . . . I mean, they will make me *ku-jat*, put me out of the panch. You better think it over, Dais, and save me from all this trouble. Look, I give them me word that you will turn a Hindu.'

She turned another searching look on Gurudeva, and said, briefly and explicitly:

'You must be nuts too! You and the set of you!'

Gurudeva opened his eyes wide.

Daisy added: 'Me? Turn Hindu? Ha! Man, don't make me laugh. Me wear *ghungri* and *orhani* and *chappals* and long hair? Me give up rouge and lipstick? You can all go to hell.'

'I see,' said Gurudeva, vexed now, and thunderstruck. 'And if you kian't do as I say, you better go too.'

'Hell with you!' said Daisy.

And she went before the little mirror she had set up against the wall in Gurudeva's room – which was all the room she had – and began to fix her hair. Leaving Gurudeva outside, she banged the door shut; in ten minutes she had changed into fresh clothes; then went to work with powder, rouge and lipstick; then packed her suitcase and flew out of the room, to catch the late bus to Port of Spain.

Gurudeva, old Jaimungal and, in fact, all the other members of the household, stood against the veranda rail and watched her go – to all but Gurudeva, the embodiment of an evil thing leaving them at last.

Quietly and sadly Gurudeva said to the old man:

'So you see, Bap, once mo' I is a bachelor again.' He meditated a moment, then said, more to himself than to anyone else: 'Look to me I was born not to have a son.'

'Yes, *beta*,' said Jaimungal; then, catching himself, said quickly, 'No, *beta*.'

Jhulani said: 'Leh she go, *beta*; you goin' get plenty more.'

'Yes, Mai,' said Gurudeva.